LOVE
IS A
REVOLUTION

ALSO BY RENÉE WATSON

Watch Us Rise (with Ellen Hagan)
Piecing Me Together
This Side of Home
What Momma Left Me

FOR YOUNGER READERS

Ways to Make Sunshine
Some Places More Than Others

LOVE
IS A
REVOLUTION

RENÉE WATSON

BLOOMSBURY
NEW YORK   LONDON   OXFORD   NEW DELHI   SYDNEY

WITHDRAWN

BLOOMSBURY YA
Bloomsbury Publishing Inc., part of Bloomsbury Publishing Plc
1385 Broadway, New York, NY 10018

BLOOMSBURY and the Diana logo are trademarks of Bloomsbury Publishing Plc

First published in the United States of America in February 2021
by Bloomsbury Children's Books

Bloomsbury books may be purchased for business or promotional use.
For information on bulk purchases please contact Macmillan Corporate and
Premium Sales Department at specialmarkets@macmillan.com

Library of Congress Cataloging-in-Publication Data
Names: Watson, Renée, author.
Title: Love is a revolution / by Renée Watson.
Description: New York : Bloomsbury, 2021.
Summary: Harlem teenager Nala is looking forward
to a summer of movies and ice cream until she falls in love with
the very woke Tye and pretends to be a social activist.
Identifiers: LCCN 2020035010 (print) | LCCN 2020035011 (e-book)
ISBN 978-1-5476-0060-1 (hardcover) • ISBN 978-1-5476-0061-8 (e-book)
Subjects: CYAC: Love—Fiction. | Dating (Social customs)—Fiction. |
Self-acceptance—Fiction. | Social action—Fiction. | Jamaican Americans—Fiction. |
Harlem (New York, N.Y.)—Fiction. | New York (N.Y.)—Fiction.
Classification: LCC PZ7.W32868 Lo 2021 (print) |
LCC PZ7.W32868 (e-book) | DDC [Fic]—dc23
LC record available at https://lccn.loc.gov/2020035010
LC e-book record available at https://lccn.loc.gov/2020035011

Book design by Jeanette Levy
Typeset by Westchester Publishing Services
Printed and bound in the U.S.A. by Berryville Graphics Inc., Berryville, Virginia
2 4 6 8 10 9 7 5 3 1

All papers used by Bloomsbury Publishing Plc are natural, recyclable products
made from wood grown in well-managed forests. The manufacturing processes
conform to the environmental regulations of the country of origin.

To find out more about our authors and books visit www.bloomsbury.com
and sign up for our newsletters.

Revolution is not a one-time event . . . or something that happens around us rather than inside of us.
—Audre Lorde

LOVE
IS A
REVOLUTION

1

3 THINGS I WANT TO DO THIS SUMMER

1. Find a new hairstyle. According to Grandma, hair is a Black girl's crown. The thicker and longer the better, so I definitely won't cut it. But I like to experiment: perm it, dye it, weave it, wig it. This summer, I want to do something I haven't done before. Maybe I'll get highlights—chestnut ombré or copper brown. Maybe honey blonde. Subtle of course, just enough to add texture and depth.

2. Find time to spend with Imani, my cousin-sister-friend. We have a plan to hang out with our best friend, Sadie, and binge-watch everything on Netflix that we've been putting off because of too much schoolwork. We have a long, long list,

but it's not all senseless entertainment. There are a few documentaries on there too—music docu-series about some of our favorite singers— but still, it's informative and educational. So our brains will be learning something.

3. (And this is the most important) Find love.

And I want to find love because I want someone's hand to hold as we roam Harlem's summer streets. I want to find love because I am tired of being the fifth wheel with Imani and Asher, who act like they're married, and Sadie and Jackson, who swear they're not a couple but are always (no, really, *always*) together. It's the last week of June and the first weekend of summer break. We're just months away from being seniors, and I have only had one boyfriend—if I can even call him that. He moved to Philly after just one month of us making it official. And I know New York and Philly aren't oceans apart, but they're not around the corner either. We both thought it was too much of a distance for us to make it work. And I want to find love because now I don't have a date for winter formal, or the prom.

And I want to find love because . . . who doesn't? Who doesn't want someone to laugh with even when something is corny and only funny if you know the inside joke? Who doesn't want someone to call at night and talk about tiny things like *what are you doing?* and *want to get something to eat?* And big things like *what's the one thing you want to do before you die?* and *what are you afraid of?* and *who do you want to be in the world?*

I want that.

But right now, it's not about what I want. Right now it's all about Imani, my cousin-sister-friend. It's her birthday, and I promised we could do whatever she wants. And of all the things Imani could want for her birthday, she jumps up off her bed and says, "Nala, do you want to come with me to the talent show tonight?

What I really want to say is *absolutely not.* First of all, it's raining. All of Harlem is drenched and somber. It would be one thing if it was just regular rain. But no. This is hot New York summer rain. This is a steamy downpour that just makes the air even more muggy and humid. What am I going to do with my hair tonight?

But a promise is a promise, so I get dressed and agree to venture out in this hotter-than-a-sauna storm because I'd do anything for Imani, my cousin-sister-friend, who shares her mom and dad with me. I've been living here since I was thirteen, when I got into a fight with Mom and I stormed out to spend the night at Aunt Ebony's and I've been living here ever since. I'm seventeen now. Six months younger than Imani, and she never lets me forget it, as if being six months older than me really counts. There is no mistaking that we are family.

Whenever we go to Jamaica to visit our relatives, people we don't even know come up to us, saying, "You must be one of the Robertsons." Some people even think we're sisters—we look just like our mommas, who look just like each other. Strong genes, Grandma always says. Imani and I are what Grandma calls big boned. That's in our genes too. Imani always rolls her eyes whenever Grandma uses any other phrase for "fat" except the word "fat." "It's not a bad word unless you use it in a bad way," Imani always says. "I'm fat. It's just a description. It doesn't have to cast negative judgment."

And this is where we differ. I am not down with the Say-It-Loud-I'm-Fat-and-I'm-Proud movement. I don't have low self-esteem or anything, I just don't feel the need to talk about my weight or make statements about it or reclaim a word that was never mine in the first place.

I sit on Imani's bed. "So tell me what's going to happen tonight."

"A talent show," she says. Imani dabs her wrists with an oil she bought from a street vendor on 125th. I can hardly smell it, it's so soft. Then she pulls her chunky braids up in

4

a ponytail. Sadie did her hair two days ago so it still has that I-just-got-my-hair-done look.

"What's the prize?" I ask.

"I don't know. A trophy, maybe. Or a certificate. I can't remember. But who wins isn't important," Imani says.

"Easy for you to say. Tell that to the performers."

"Well, what I mean is, it's a talent show to raise money and awareness. It will be promoting Inspire Harlem and raising money for our activism programs," she says. "So it's more about the gathering and being together and raising money than someone winning a prize."

I try really hard not to roll my eyes. "So, this is how you want to spend your birthday? At an Inspire Harlem talent show?"

"Don't start with me, Nala. You asked me what I want to do and this is what I want to do. We're going to Harlem Shake afterward. Does that make it better for you?"

"It's not about me. It's about what you want," I say. I mostly mean it.

"It's never about what I want," Imani mumbles.

She thinks I didn't hear her, but I did. I definitely did. "What is that supposed to mean?" I ask.

She ignores my question and keeps talking. "I don't know why you don't like my Inspire Harlem friends."

"I like them," I say. And then I mumble just like she

5

did, but softer to make sure she doesn't hear me. "They don't like me."

And here is Reason Number Two why I don't want to go: Imani and her Inspire Harlem friends. Inspire Harlem is an organization for Harlem teens that does community service projects and hosts awareness events about various social issues. Imani has been trying to get me to join for the past year. But I don't know, they're a little too . . . well, let's just say I don't think I'm a good fit.

The last Inspire Harlem event I went to was an open mic. The theme was Love Is Love. I thought it would be a night of love poems, sweet and beautiful sentiments about relationships with parents, partners, friends. But no. The first poem was an I-Love-to-Hate-You poem recited by a girl who wrote a poem to her ex-girlfriend. There were poems about loving people even though they aren't worthy of love and poems about how America doesn't love Black people, or Native people, or immigrants, or women.

It was not the Roses-Are Red-Violets-Are-Blue kind of poems I am used to.

And I should have known it would be that way. All the teens in Inspire Harlem are activists, which sometimes feels like a word that means their opinion is the only one that matters. I guess I just don't know if I could live up to the standards they have.

Just last night, Imani went through the junk drawer in the kitchen and threw out all the plastic straws Uncle Randy has been saving from delivery and takeout. "Isn't throwing away the unused straws just as bad as if I had used them and then thrown them away?" he asked.

She didn't have an answer for that.

And now she's on this I-only-take-five-minute-showers movement, and I'm all for her setting that as her own personal goal, but I like my warm, long showers and I don't need her shaking her head in disapproval every time I come out of the bathroom.

"All right, I'm going to get ready," I say. I walk through the passageway that connects our rooms. The alcove has drawers and cabinets on both sides—extra storage and closet space for all our stuff that Aunt Ebony keeps saying we need to go through so we can give away clothes we don't wear anymore.

As soon as I get in my room, I turn on music. I've found a new favorite artist, Bluc, a Jamaican singer who mixes reggae and R&B. She's twenty-one and she's big, like me—or as Imani would proudly say, *fat*. I've been listening to her music nonstop. I have just finished putting my jeans on when Imani barges into my room. "I knocked, but you can't hear me with that music so loud," she says. She turns it down just a little. "I mean, I'm a fan too, but really? You've had the song on repeat all day."

"This from the queen of rewatching movies and saying the lines with the characters."

"Fair," Imani says. "Absolutely fair." We laugh, and then she closes my door so she can look at herself in the full-length mirror that hangs on the back. "I need your help. Which shirt should I wear?" Imani asks. Right now she only has on jeans and her bra. In her left hand she is holding a shirt that says, I Am My Ancestors' Wildest Dreams, and in her right hand, a shirt with a drawing of a closed fist raised and the word Resist under it. Both are black with white lettering.

"That one." I point to her left hand.

"Thanks." Imani puts the shirt on and comes over to my dresser to skim through my jewelry. We are always in and out of each other's rooms borrowing and swapping.

Now I am second-guessing my outfit. My green sundress seems too dressy and doesn't make any kind of statement. I look through my closet. I only own one graphic tee, and it says I Woke Up Like This. I'm pretty sure this isn't the shirt to wear around this activist crowd. I change into a black V-neck and jeans. I'll make it more stylish by adding some necklaces and bracelets. Aunt Liz taught me that accessories are the key to every outfit.

Imani has picked through all my bracelets and chooses the chunky silver one. She looks in the mirror. "You ready?"

"Do I look ready?" I point to my face that has no makeup, to my hair that is still wrapped in a scarf. "I need at least fifteen minutes." I plug in my flat iron, turn the dial up to the highest heat.

"We don't have fifteen minutes. Be ready in five."

"Ten," I call out. "Beauty takes time."

"Makeup doesn't make you beautiful."

"No, but it enhances it," I say. I pick up a tube of lipstick and hold it out toward Imani. "This color would look so good on you. You should let me do your makeup one day."

"Five minutes, Nala. I'll be downstairs."

"I can't do nine steps in five minutes."

"Nine steps? Are you serious?" Imani's footsteps echo in the hallway as she runs down the stairs. "You better hurry up."

"And now it'll be twelve minutes since you kept talking to me." I laugh and begin my makeup routine. For me, the key to wearing makeup is making it look like I don't have any on.

9 STEPS FOR APPLYING MAKEUP

1. Primer. Because I have to make sure the foundation powder goes on smoothly.

2. Eyebrows. I use an eyebrow pencil to define my arch and make my brows full. They're already kind of thick, so I don't need to do too much.

3. Foundation. It took me a while to find the perfect match for my dark skin, but about a month ago Aunt Liz took me makeup shopping and we did a color-matching test, so now I know the perfect shade to use.

4. Blush. Yes, I wear blush. A warm brown blush so my face doesn't look so flat.

5. Eye shadow. Less is more. I do use color, but on a day like today, I'm keeping it simple.

6. Eyeliner. I use a felt tip. It goes on easier and doesn't smudge like pencil. I'm going for that evening smoky eye—it'll elevate this outfit I'm wearing.

7. Mascara. I'm not a fan of wearing so much mascara that it looks like spiders are crawling out of my eyes, but I do lay it on thick so I can have full, fluttering lashes.

8. Lipstick/Lip gloss. Sometimes I wear both,
   depending on the color and texture. Tonight, I'm
   doing lipstick. Even though it's gray outside,
   I'm going with a bright berry color for summer.

9. Look at myself in the mirror. I just sit and stare
   for one whole minute. Take in this beauty
   that everyone else will be seeing, make sure
   everything is just right.

And that's it. My face is complete.

Next, I touch up my hair with my flat iron, making sure my edges are straight. Since it's raining so hard, I pull it up in a sloppy-on-purpose ponytail, and as promised, twelve minutes have passed and I'm ready to go.

Just as I am pulling the plug out of the socket, Imani calls out to me. "Nala, we're going to be late! Come on."

"Coming." I grab my umbrella.

When I get downstairs, Imani is in the kitchen at the sink filling her metal water bottle. Uncle Randy and Aunt Ebony are here cooking together, and the way they have this kitchen smelling with sweet plantains and curry chicken makes me want to stay and eat dinner.

"Save some for me," I say. I kiss Aunt Ebony on her cheek.

"Oh, don't worry, I'm sure we'll be eating this chicken for the next few days. I'm making enough to last. Too hot to keep turning this stove on. Plus, I'm on summer vacation too, so that should mean I get a break from cooking." Aunt Ebony says this even though we all know she'll be back in the kitchen tomorrow cooking up something delicious and taking a plate over to Grandma. She is the oldest of Grandma's daughters. Her and Uncle Randy married in their last year of college. So even though they have been married for a long time, they are younger than the parents of a lot of my friends. Aunt Ebony teaches at an elementary school just a few blocks down the street, so it's summer break for her too.

Aunt Liz is two years younger and lives in a condo on 116th. She's a personal stylist and has a lot of famous clients. Aunt Liz is always, always dressed like she's going to be in a photo shoot. Even her pajamas are photo worthy.

And then there's my mom. She's the youngest, the only one who has a job and not a career. She's worked at clothing stores, restaurants, offices. They were all born in Spanish Town, the parish of St. Catherine, and moved to New York in their teens when Grandpa decided that the States would give his children a better life. Grandma says he was a man whose dreams wouldn't let him sleep. She'd wake up in the middle of the night, and he'd be at the kitchen table working on a job application or writing out goals for the family.

Grandpa loved living in New York, but his heart was in Spanish Town. He went back to Jamaica at least twice a year. Grandma has tried to keep the tradition. We all go once a year, usually for Christmas since that's when Aunt Ebony is off from work. When we go, we stay in Kingston because that's where most of the family lives now.

Before Imani and I leave we have to go through our goodbye routine with Aunt Ebony and Uncle Randy: Where are you going? Who else is going to be there? When will you be back?

We leave and on our way to the library, I tell Imani, "We should have invited Sadie."

"Oh, she'll be there. She's a member of Inspire Harlem now."

"She is?" I ask.

"Yeah, I finally convinced her to join."

Sadie is in Inspire Harlem now. Why didn't I know this?

Because we are running late, Imani is speed walking, which is hard to do in pouring-down rain. The puddles are splashing, and I am drenched. We don't say much to each other on the way to the library. Mostly because we are walking fast and are out of breath, but also because I can't stop thinking about Sadie joining Inspire Harlem. Sadie usually agrees with me about Imani and her woke friends. The two of us tease Imani all the time, calling her Angela Davis Jr., and when we really want to get under her skin, we respond with "Yes, ma'am" when she's being bossy or nagging us about throwing something in the trash that should be recycled.

Maybe it's petty to be thinking like this, but I really don't want to go to this talent show tonight. Normally when I go to an Inspire Harlem event, Sadie and I sit together. We whisper our commentary to each other about everything that's happening. We nudge each other whenever someone says a corny Save-the-World mantra or cliché. We clear our throats as a signal that it's time to leave. There's always been a *we*—me and Sadie—at these events, with our own inside jokes. Me and Sadie telling Imani that the issues she cares about are serious but not *that* serious. Imani is my cousin-sister-friend, and Sadie is my best friend.

They are my *we*.

But now that Sadie has joined Inspire Harlem, who will I have?

2

5 REASONS I HATE THE RAIN

1. It makes my hair poof out into an Afro. And accidental Afros are not cute. At all.

2. It makes walking in New York a hazardous activity. Umbrellas bumping and clashing against shoulders and heads as we all squeeze past one another. (Why do people keep their umbrellas up even when walking under scaffolding?)

3. It makes the trash on the street smell even worse, and is there anything worse than the smell of wet garbage?

4. It settles into deep puddles at corners, and cars speed by, splashing me like I'm on a water park

ride. Except I'm not. There is nothing refreshing
or fun about this water.

5. It paints the sky gray, and gray skies remind
   me of the day I left Mom's house—a storm of
   another kind. The sky was gray that day, and the
   rain was angry and it soaked my clothes, my
   bags, my shoes, and by the time I walked to
   Imani's house my face was wet from rain and
   snot and tears.

The talent show is held at the library on Lenox and 136th Street. Even though it's just a short walk from our brownstone, by the time we get there we look like we've been playing in a dunk tank. But most people here are soaked too, so it kind of doesn't matter. We put our umbrellas in a bucket at the door and go into the community room. There's music playing and the lights are dim. The one thing I can say about Inspire Harlem events is that they always have good music and good food. They also know how to transform a regular room into a space that makes you want to hang out, stay awhile. Normally this room is kind of bland, but tonight there's special lighting that sets a mood like we're at a real show at some nice theater downtown.

As soon as we step inside, people start crowding around Imani, hugging her and wishing her a happy birthday. Sadie hugs her first, then comes over to me and before I can even say hello, she is apologizing and looking at me with guilt in her eyes. "Don't be mad at me, okay?"

"Traitor," I say.

"I know. I know. But my mom told me I had to do something this summer. So it was either this or work at our family's candy store. And you know I'm not doing that." Sadie moves her long braids from the right to left. "Come with me. I'm sitting over there." Sadie points to the front row and starts walking.

The front row? *We* never sit that close up.

As soon as we sit down, Toya Perkins walks over. She struts in like a peacock. Head held high, showing off her undeniable beauty. Today, she is wearing a jean skirt with a black T-shirt that has the year 1619 in the center of her chest. A patterned wrap crowns her head. I've been to at least twenty Inspire Harlem events, but every time she sees me, she introduces herself like we've never met. She is carrying two clipboards in her hand, and when she gets in front of us, she hands one to Sadie and says, "You can't sit down yet, we're working the event. We need you to greet people and get them to sign up for the newsletter."

17

Sadie takes the clipboard and looks it over. "Oh, uh, sorry, I didn't know I needed to do this. I thought I was on the cleanup committee."

"We're all on the cleanup committee." Toya reaches in her pocket and pulls out a pen. "Here, make sure you give it back." Before walking away, she looks at me and says, "And hello, my name is LaToya. You look familiar."

"We've met. I'm Nala."

"Welcome, I hope you enjoy tonight's show." Toya shakes my hand and walks away.

Once Sadie is sure Toya is far enough away, she rolls her eyes. Then, she puts a fake smile on and holds the clipboard out to me. "Would you like to sign up?"

I play along. "For?"

Sadie puts on a telemarketing voice. "Our e-blast list. We send out a newsletter once a month. It's just a way for you to keep up with all our events and an occasional call to action."

"Oh, um, no—no thank you," I say.

Sadie says, "Suit yourself. But don't be mad when you realize you've missed the announcement on tips for fighting climate change. It's a must read." I know she's just messing with me when she says this, and it feels good to know that even though now she is one of them, she is still a part of my *we.*

Just when Sadie is about to walk away, here comes Toya

again, hovering and clearly eavesdropping. "Did you need something?" Sadie asks, because she is not the type of person to let people go unchecked.

"Oh, no, I was just taking everything in. I mean, isn't it such a powerful thing to be here in this sacred space?"

I smile because what else am I supposed to do? I have no idea why Toya is calling this library sacred. Maybe she says this about all libraries. Maybe she loves books. Sadie doesn't seem to get it either. We both just look at Toya, faces blank.

Toya must realize that we don't have a clue about what she's referring to. She lowers her voice. "You do know where you are, don't you? This is the Countee Cullen Library."

"Oh," I say.

But not dramatic or heartfelt enough, because she goes on. "You know, Countee Cullen . . . the Harlem Renaissance poet . . . the teacher?"

I got nothing.

Sadie nods, but I think she is just nodding to make Toya stop talking.

"Before the library was built, A'Lelia Walker's townhouse was here. You know, A'Lelia Walker—the daughter of Madam C. J. Walker? She opened her home as a gathering space for writers during the Harlem Renaissance, and now it's this library."

Note to self: Look up Countee Cullen and Madam C. J. Walker.

"Sadie, we should mingle. We need to get more sign-ups," Toya says. "Nala, are you coming with us to Harlem Shake? We're all going out later to celebrate Imani. Wait, you're her cousin, right?"

Of course I'm going, and you know that we are related. Imani is *my* cousin-sister-friend. Why wouldn't I be there?

I nod.

"Perfect," she says.

The lights flicker, giving everyone a sign that the show is about to start. So much for them signing up more people. Sadie sits next to me, and the first two rows fill up with Inspire Harlem teens. I notice that just about everyone sitting in this section is wearing a graphic tee that has some kind of statement on it or the face of someone important. I recognize two of the faces. Malcolm X and Maya Angelou. The rest, I have no idea.

Maybe one of them is Countee Cullen.

Imani walks over to us and sits next to me, in the middle of her birthday crew. The lights dim even more, and once it is completely blacked out, there is cheering and clapping. The stage lights are too dark at first, so I can't really see the person talking. "Good evening, everyone. We're here tonight to remember Harlem, to honor Harlem, to critique Harlem, to love Harlem . . . we're here tonight to Inspire Harlem."

There are shouts and whistles and so much clapping.

Then, finally, the lights rise.

And I see him.

"My name is Tye Brown, and I will be your host for the evening." While everyone is still clapping, he says, "Tonight's going to be a special night," and then I swear he looks at me and says, "Sit back and enjoy." I almost yell out *I will! Oh, I will!* but I keep it together and settle into my seat.

I whisper to Imani, "Who is he? I've never seen him before."

"Tye. He's new," she says.

And I turn to Sadie and whisper, "I mean, if I had known guys like that were a part of this, maybe I would have joined too."

Sadie laughs.

"Shh!" Imani scolds us.

I sit back, give my full attention to Tye. He explains what Inspire Harlem is and talks us through how the night will go. Then, his voice gets serious and he says, "Singer and activist Nina Simone said, 'It's an artist's duty to reflect the times in which we live.' This isn't your typical talent show. Each act has thought about the message in their art, the mission behind their performance."

A few people clap when he says this.

"This is a supportive, brave space—please only show love for everyone who has the courage to come to the stage," Tye says. And then, he smiles the most gorgeous smile I have ever seen and says, "Let's begin."

I don't believe in love at first sight. I don't even know if I believe that there's such a thing as a soul mate or one true love. But right now, in this moment, I am ready to profess my love for Tye Brown.

Okay, fine, I don't really love him. I don't know him (yet), but there are some things I know about him in just the first thirty minutes of the talent show, and those things, I love.

3 THINGS I ALREADY LOVE ABOUT TYE BROWN

1. I love his dark skin. The way his white shirt contrasts against his deep brown complexion. I love his style. How his shirt has the letters *B L A C K* across his chest, making him a living poem.

2. I love the way his deep voice bellows out, filling up the space, how his voice is electric shock

waves when he needs to amp up the crowd, how
it is a warm hug when he welcomes each person
to the stage.

3. I love that when the fourth person gets choked up
with tears because he can't remember the lyrics
to his rap, Tye comes from backstage and stands
next to him, putting his hand on his shoulder.
I love how they just stand there for a whole minute
and the audience is silent, how Tye asks, "Do you
want to start over?" I love how Tye stands there
while the boy performs, never leaving his side,
bobbing his head and moving to the beat.

Yeah, those are the things I love about Tye. It was definitely worth coming out in the rain tonight.

The next person up is a girl named Gabby. Her hair is
pulled back in a neat ponytail, and I can't tell if the glasses
she is wearing are for necessity or fashion. She sings a
song she wrote just for this event, and that alone should
make her the winner. I feel sorry for the people coming
after her.

The next performance is a group of steppers. They
have the crowed hyped. By the time they are done, I think
maybe they might beat Gabby. But if they do, it'll be close.
I completely tune out during the next act. A girl is singing

some type of Heal-the-World song, and I am bored and barely listening to her. It's not that she can't sing—the song is just corny. To me anyway. All I am thinking about is when will Tye be coming back to the stage. But once the girl stops singing, the lights come up for a short intermission.

Most people rush to the bathrooms. I walk over to the snack table—I want to get something to drink and also, I see that Tye is standing over there. I am trying to think of something to say to him, but I can't even get my mouth to open. Up close he is even more handsome and now I can smell his cologne. I just want to run away and look at him from across the room.

"Enjoying the show?" Tye asks. He is talking to me. To me.

"Um, yes, I—I'm really, yes, I'm enjoying it." *Get it together, Nala Robertson. Come on.*

"Are you new to Inspire Harlem?"

"Oh, no. I'm not a part of it. Hi, I'm Nala. Imani is my cousin. She invited me."

"Oh, Imani? That's my girl. I'm Tye." He shakes my hand, which I think is kind of formal, but holding his hand feels like holding silk and I want to hold on to him and never let him go. Tye lets go and fills his water bottle. He takes a long drink.

Say something, Nala. Say something. "Inspire Harlem is a great program. Imani really likes being in it."

"Yeah. I love it so far. I'm excited about what we've planned for this summer. Did Imani tell you about it?"

"No," I say. But of course she did. I just want to keep talking to him.

"All summer long we'll be having awareness events— I'm the team leader for our community block party. You should come," Tye says. I have never heard someone sound so excited about a community service project. Tye steps away from the table because we're holding the line up. I realize I don't even have anything in my hand, no water or plate of veggies and dip to play it off like I didn't just come over here to talk with him. "What about you? What are you up to this summer?" he asks.

"Oh, I'm, um, I'm . . . I volunteer for an organization that offers activities for elderly people in the neighborhood. We do, um, like arts and crafts stuff with them—nothing super important or at the magnitude of Inspire Harlem," I say. He doesn't need to know that really, I am just talking about the one time last month when I spent the day at Grandma's helping her put a puzzle together.

"That's great that you're doing that," Tye says.

"Yeah, some of them don't have family that come visit and just need to get out of their apartments and do some- thing. We do all kinds of activities with them."

"Like what?"

"Um, well, like I mentioned, arts and crafts . . . um,

knitting. We also have story time, not like kindergarten story time, but I read novels to them and sometimes we just play games and build puzzles."

All of this is a true-lie.

I've done these things with Grandma and her friends. Just not with a formal group of people or with an organization. But I had to say something. I mean, I couldn't tell him that I'm spending my summer watching Netflix and trying out the summer flavors of ice cream at Sugar Hill Creamery.

Ms. Lori, the director of Inspire Harlem, walks over to us. "Tye, we're just about ready to start the second half," she says. "Five minutes."

"Okay." Tye refills his water bottle one more time. "Nice to meet you, Nala," he says. "Are you coming to hang with us afterward?"

"At Harlem Shake? Yes. I wouldn't miss celebrating Imani's birthday, plus, they have the best burgers," I say.

"One of the best veggie burgers in the city."

Veggie? Is he vegetarian? I think of something to say. "Yeah. It's so hard to find good vegetarian food." And by that I mean, most vegetarian food is the absolute worst food ever.

"Oh, you're vegetarian?" Tye asks.

I give a slow yes. A yes that's a lie with no truth in it at all.

"I'm a pescatarian," he tells me.

"A what?"

"I eat fish," he says.

"Oh yeah, me too," I say.

"So, you're not a vegetarian?"

I clear my throat. "I'm a vegetarian who's sometimes a pescatarian." *Stop the lies, Nala. Stop it.*

Ms. Lori comes back over and tells Tye it's time to start.

"It was nice to meet you, Nala. I gotta go. But we'll talk more. Harlem Shake?"

"Yes, I'll be there," I say. "And nice to meet you too. You're a really good host. I'm glad I came tonight."

And this is not a lie.

3

By the time we leave the library, the rain has stopped. It's still muggy, so I keep my hair in a ponytail because the last thing I need is to look like a Black Chia Pet. The sun has faded into the clouds, and the city lights twinkle like stars, lighting our way down Lenox Ave as we walk to Harlem Shake. Imani and Sadie are leading the way. Imani is carrying the flowers Toya gave her, so it probably looks like we are her entourage or that she is some kind of princess and we are her court. The sidewalks uptown are wide, but still, with this many out on a summer Friday night, I have to manuver my way to keep up with the group. I try to walk next to Tye, but Toya has her arm linked with his like she is his buddy for the night. "You were so good tonight, Tye," she says. "I'm so glad you've joined Inspire Harlem."

"Thanks," Tye says. Then he turns around and sees me behind them. "You good, Nala?" He steps to the side, breaking arms with Toya to make room for me. I step in the middle of them, and Toya makes a face that is definitely not the warm, friendly smile she greeted me with earlier.

When we get to the restuarant, there's not enough space for us all, so we push two tables together. Tye and I sit next to each other, and Toya sits across from him. Imani is across from me next to Asher. Sadie and Jackson are at the counter ordering their food. A girl named Lynn is with them. Lynn has been to the house a few times, mostly for Inspire Harlem meetings. She wears her hair low to her scalp and always has the biggest hoop earrings on. Every time I see her, I think we should go shopping together. I like her style.

Tye stands and says to me, "Tell me what you want and I'll get it."

I want you.

"Um, let me see," I say. And I look the menu over. I already know what I want—the Hot Mess Burger. This deliciousness is two hamburger patties, onions, pickles, and special sauce, topped with pickled cherry pepper, bacon relish, American cheese, and smoky chipotle mayonnaise. But I have to keep up my vegetarian diet in front of Tye. There is nothing else on this menu that I want. I refuse to get a kale salad at a burger joint. And I've had a veggie burger once. Well, I should say I tasted a veggie burger. One bite and I threw the rest away. "I think I'll just get a side of fries," I tell Tye.

"Are you sure?"

"Um . . . and a chocolate milkshake," I say, even though I really want to go ahead and add the burger. I have only known Tye for a few hours, and already I am giving up a lot for him.

Toya says, "I'm getting the veggie burger, but I'll go up with you. I have a few special requests, so I'll just order it myself." She stands from the table and walks with Tye to the counter. I watch them standing next to each other and see how when Toya laughs, she leans into Tye, holds on to his arm like she needs him to keep her standing. It takes them a while, but finally they come back to the table with our food. They both have veggie burgers, Toya's with extra pickles, sourdough bread instead of the bun, and a side of special sauce. They both have sweet potato fries. I slowly eat mine, the whole time imagining I was eating a steak.

It could be worse. Tye could be vegan.

TOP 3 FOODS I CAN'T LIVE WITHOUT

1. Meat: goat, beef, pork, chicken, lamb, duck.
   Prepared all ways: grilled, fried, baked, stewed,

seared, braised. On a stick, on the bone, off the bone, shredded, chunk, sliced, ground. It's not a meal if there's no meat.

2. Ice cream. Imagine it, no hot fudge sundaes or thick scoops of strawberry packed in a waffle cone. Only watery, cold globs pretending to be dessert worth eating. And let's be clear—this goes for sorbet and gelato and frozen yogurt and smoothies too. There is nothing—absolutely nothing—as good as the real thing. If you want ice cream, nothing else will do.

3. Cheese. Cheese makes everything better. Burgers, sandwiches, scrambled eggs, crackers, bread. My specialty to make is a grilled cheese sandwich. And cheese is good all by itself. Ever had string cheese for a snack? Ever had melted cheese ooze onto the wrapper of a burger? That's the best part sometimes—savoring every single bit of it. And I know there are cheese substitutes. But does vegan cheese even melt the same way? Does is stretch like an accordian when you pull a slice of pizza from the box? No. I don't think so.

We are just about finished eating, and the restaurant isn't as crowded now that it's late into the night. We spread out and take up even more space. Then, Sadie says, "Okay, Birthday Girl, it's time for your song." We sing "Happy Birthday" to Imani the traditional way and then Stevie's version. The whole restaurant joins in because this is Harlem and strangers have no problem joining in on a celebration. I try not to laugh at Imani, who is struggling to drink her thick milkshake without a straw. It keeps getting on her nose, but she refuses to get a straw, not even the paper ones that are there as an alternative. Toya has one of those, but she can't drink through it because the shake is too thick, so she is letting it sit for a while to thin out.

Imani sets her shake down and says, "So, anyone notice the songs on the playlist that Marcy put together for tonight's intermission? Ms. Lori is going to have something to say about that, for sure."

Toya nods her head, eating the last bit of her fries. "Oh my goodness. I was so embarrassed. What was Marcy thinking?"

"What was wrong with the music tonight?" I ask. And why did I ask that? All of them look at me like I have just asked the most ridiculous question. Except for Sadie. Sadie and I have similar taste in music and movies, so most of our conversations start with *have you seen?* or *have you heard?*

Toya says, "First of all, our name is Inspire Harlem, so maybe it would have been a good idea to have some kind of inspirational songs. Not songs with vulgar lyrics that actually undermine the work we are trying to do and all we stand for."

Sadie gives me a look, telling me not to push it. I should take her advice and just let them talk because I am not a part of Inspire Harlem so why should I care, but for some reason I keep talking. "But all the songs were edited versions. What's the—"

"If it needs to be an edited version, maybe it doesn't need to be played," Lynn says.

That sounds like something my grandmother would say.

"It's okay, Nala, you wouldn't understand," Imani says.

"What is that supposed to mean?"

"Well, we . . . being a part of Inspire Harlem means we've had to take workshops about how to read the media and how to see all the messages that music, commericals, and even the news are sending to us."

Lynn jumps in, as if I need more explanation. "We've discussed how capitalism has made us go after things that we don't need and how music sometimes reinforces those toxic ideals."

And now Toya wants to teach me something. "So, like, it's not just the music, but the videos and everything that goes into the production of it—think about how the women in those videos look. It's very rare that a woman has natural hair or is big—"

"As in fat, not thick," Imani adds.

"Right, so you know—like you straightening your hair, wearing makeup, all your life you've been given messages telling you that you have to do that to be beautiful. I get it. I used to be the same way. But when you know better, you do better."

"Or, when you have freedom, you are free to do what you want with your body and your hair," I say. And I didn't need a special program to tell me that.

"All right, can we just . . . let's talk about something else," Sadie says finally.

"Yeah, let's drop it." Imani looks at me, an apology in her eyes.

I look away.

"I didn't mean to start anything," Imani says.

But there is no stopping because Toya has more to say. She keeps going on about how the songs on Marcy's playlist were reinforcing harmful beauty standards and full of misogynistic lyrics.

Sadie rolls her eyes and I smile at her. I know at least two songs that were played tonight are songs Sadie loves. At least someone at this table agrees with me.

Tye, Asher, and Jackson haven't said anything.

"You don't have an opinion on this?" I ask them.

"I'm just trying to listen more. I wanted you all to speak first," Asher says, pointing to us girls. He puts his hand on Imani's leg; she scoots closer to him and rests her head on his shoulder.

I feel like maybe there's a hidden camera somewhere and at any moment they are all going to start laughing and tell me they are just kidding. That this is some kind of social justice How Woke Are You? prank. But no. Asher continues. "I've been raised on those images and lyrics, and yeah, they are degrading to women. Even the edited versions. I'm not going to lie, I still listen to problematic songs but not as much as I used to, and I definitely wouldn't have played that mix at the event we had tonight."

Tye nods. "I'm surprised Ms. Lori let it go on."

Jackson doesn't say anything, and I think it's because he disagrees or maybe doesn't have a strong opinion either way. He just keeps eating, keeping his mouth full so he doesn't have to talk.

Toya balls her napkin up and puts it on top of her half-eaten burger. "You should join Inspire Harlem, Nala. You'd learn a lot."

Not if it's going to stop me from listening to all the music I love. No thank you.

I lean back and force an *I'll think about it* smile. And then Sadie changes the subject, and they all start gossiping about Inspire Harlem drama—who wasn't there tonight, who might be getting kicked out of the program because they haven't completed enough community service hours.

I don't think I've said a word for the past fifteen minutes so I pull out my phone and pretend to be looking at something important. I can't even read what's on my screen because all I can think about is what Imani said, how she's been treating me like just because I disagree with her on certain things means I don't understand. If it wasn't her birthday, I'd get up and leave. And we still haven't talked about what she meant when she said, *"It's never about what I want."* What did she mean by that?

Tye scoots closer to me, snatches my phone out of my hands. "Are you always this quiet?"

"No. It's just that no one is talking to me." I grab my phone back.

"Sorry. They just tend to get caught up with Inspire Harlem stuff when we're all together. It took me a while to feel a part of the group too."

Who said I'm trying to be a part of this group?

"So, what do you want to talk about?" Tye asks.

I want to know if you like Toya as much as she likes you, because she clearly likes you, but I can't tell if you like her too. "Um, I don't know. That's a weird question."

"Is it?"

"Conversation should just happen naturally. I can't just come up with a topic to talk about. That feels forced."

"Okay, okay," Tye says. He is silent for just a moment and then says, "So, tell me more about the program you volunteer for. What's the name again?"

I never told you a name because there is no name. "Sugar Hill Senior Living. That's, uh, that's the name of the residence. Most of the people living there are all on their own. They cook and take care of themselves, they go as they please. But there are some who have assisted living. Anyone who lives there can attend the programs I do. It's just a small thing in the lounge. We don't have, like, an official name for it." I am talking low to make sure Imani doesn't hear me. But she is so into her conversation with everyone else, I think I am the last person on her mind.

Tye says, "What you're doing doesn't sound small to me. It's a big deal to be company for people who need it. I'm sure they love having you. You should come up with a name. That could make it even more special."

Great. I have Tye's attention, and all he can talk about is old people doing arts and crafts with me. Really?

Before I can answer him, Imani stands up. "Ready to go?" she asks, caught in a long yawn.

We all stand up and leave Harlem Shake. We've been in the air conditioning so long that I forgot how hot it is outside. We walk into Harlem's steam, and Sadie, Jackson, and Lynn are the first to say goodbye. They cross the street toward Fifth Avenue. Toya gives us all a hug but holds on to Tye the longest. She walks to the left and turns one more time to say goodbye, but I think this last wave is just to Tye.

Imani, Asher, and I head home; Tye walks with us. I walk slow on purpose, wanting to be beside Tye as long as I can. Imani is in front of us, holding hands with Asher. They've been dating for two years. At first Aunt Ebony and Uncle Randy weren't too excited about their daughter dating anyone, but Asher won them over once they realized he was just as serious about his grades and integrity as he was about having a girlfriend. Asher has become a part of the family. He's over for dinner at least once a week.

I watch them walk, hand in hand, and I wonder if I will ever have that. Imani has always had someone to love and be loved by. Always a boy flirting with her, asking her for her number. Her first kiss was when we were in the sixth grade. I remember because I was the one on lookout duty, had to make sure no teachers were walking by. The two of them had snuck off around the back of the school building while we were outside for recess. *Don't tell*, Imani said afterward.

I never did.

I want to strike up a conversation with Tye, but I don't

know what to say, so I go to the generic question I always ask when there's too much silence. "What are you thinking about?" I ask.

"Naming your program."

"What?"

"I'm trying to think of a good name. I'm pretty good at brainstorming this kind of stuff." Whenever Tye's shoulder brushes against mine, I feel an ocean flood my heart. I'd much rather talk about something more interesting. Something true. But he keeps going. "So, what if the name is a reference to the time you spend together. Like if it's an hour, it can be called the Sugar Hill Arts and Crafts Hour," Tye says. "But that's too simple. We can do better than that. That's just the first one off the dome."

"I like that idea," I play along. "What about Sugar Hill Art Studio?"

"That's better, but let's keep thinking," he says. "Maybe instead of art studio, you call it open studio since you do more than art in that space. Don't you do yoga and storytelling too?"

Oh yeah. I forgot I said that. He knows my fake program better than I do.

"I like that. What about, the Open Studio at Sugar Hill Residence?" I say.

"Perfect," Tye says. Then he asks me for my phone.

I give it to him. "I want to come check it out. Here's my number. Text me and let me know when it's okay to drop by."

And just like that I have a name for my pretend volunteer program and I'm a vegetarian. And I have the phone number of the cutest guy—and maybe the nicest—I've ever met.

I'm not sure how or if I can keep this new me up. But I sure am going to try.

4 SECRETS ABOUT IMANI THAT
I'VE NEVER TOLD

1. That Imani kissed a boy in the sixth grade at the back of the school building between the trash bins and the rusted desks that had been tossed out.

2. That Imani snuck out of the house once to meet up with Asher and came back just as the sun was waking up, just before Aunt Ebony knocked on her bedroom door to say, *Rise, shine.*

3. That sometimes Imani uses Inspire Harlem events as an excuse to spend time with Asher. Sometimes the days end earlier than she admits,

sometimes the special project she's working on is him.

4. That the day after she kissed the boy in the sixth grade, he tried to kiss me. I wouldn't let him. But I wanted to. I wanted to be wanted. Wanted to know what it felt like to be Imani for a day.

4

BLUE PLAYLIST, TRACK 1

Summer Hips

Spoken Voice: The primary function of the hip joint is to support the weight of the body in both still and active postures.

Verse 1
Sun is out, strobe light, sidewalk dance floors.
Cars driving by blasting music. Let's dance.
Move your hips, glide, slide anywhere, everywhere.

Everywhere, anywhere
being free, doin' me.
Wearin' what I want to wear.
Big body on display. This skin I'm in, so free, so me.

Hips hypnotizing, hips mesmerizing.

All this me walking down the street.

Chorus

These hips sweet.

These hips wild.

These hips steady me, carry me,

hold all my history.

Verse 2

These hips ground me when I march the streets

mourning bodies who look like me. Killed, terrorized

blatantly.

You see this Black girl dancin', think I'm sexy.

You see this Black girl dancin', think it's for you, not me.

But this dance a celebration of my story, my glory.

Chorus 2x

These hips sweet.

These hips wild.

These hips steady me, carry me,

hold all my history.

These hips sweet.

These hips wild.

These hips steady me, carry me,
hold all my history.

These hips free.
These hips free.

I can't prove it, but I think New Yorkers are happiest in the
summer. We aren't bundled up, walking fast, fast, fast to
get out of the cold, so people actually say hello, look you in
the eyes, and ask how you're doing. Music hangs off the
clouds, hovering above my head. Sometimes it's R&B,
sometimes hip-hop. Sometimes, it's merengue, Afro beats,
reggae, or soca. Depending on the neighborhood you are
walking through, you accidently walk into a family BBQ
or a neighborhood street festival. This is July, hotter than
June but not as humid as August. Now that school has
been out for a full week, it really feels like I am on a break,
and I am ready to make every day count.

Today, I am visiting Grandma. She's lived at Sugar
Hill Senior Living for a year now. She didn't want to move
here at first, but once we came and did a walk-through she
saw that it was just an apartment complex where all the residents were her age. It wasn't a place where we were throwing her away, forgetting about her. Instead, she'd still have
her independence, just with less space to have to look after

and no more brownstone stairs to climb. I think about how old Grandma is now, how it is not just about the number but the way she looks, the way she moves. She looks older, moves slower, and doesn't call us over for her last-minute family dinners as much as she used to. I miss the days when she'd call saying, "I cooked too much food—come on over and fix a plate." I miss the days when she'd call me over to teach me how to make one of her recipes, how she'd say, "I'm cooking pepper pot soup tomorrow. You want to learn how to make it?"

I think about how much longer she'll be living here on earth, not because she is sick or anything, but just because of common sense and math. She is eighty-four, so that means she has fewer years to be alive. That's just the truth, that's just math. Whenever I say this to Imani, she says I am being morbid and that I shouldn't think about that. But I think she's in denial and when Grandma really does die, Imani's going to wish she had thought about it more, that she had prepared herself.

I walk down the hallway toward Grandma's apartment, and the closer I get I hear mento music. Grandma must be cleaning. She always plays mento when she is washing dishes or straightening up. I knock on the door.

Grandma opens the door, gives me her Grandma-hug, and ushers me in. "Haven't seen none of you in a while,"

Grandma says. I see the broom leaning in the corner against the wall. Yeah, she was cleaning. "You talk to your momma lately?" Grandma wastes no time getting to the topic she wants to talk about. She doesn't ask how I'm doing, or how the weather is today—not even if I'd like something to drink. "You only have one momma, Nala. Just one."

"I know," I say. I step inside, take off my shoes, and sit on her sofa. It is covered in a slipcover hiding how old it really is. Aunt Liz offered to buy her a new one and she refused—*it still holds you up, don't it?*—she said. And so Aunt Liz bought her this floral slipcover instead.

"She hasn't called me."

"You gonna call her?" Grandma asks.

I don't answer her. She knows I won't. I think maybe her question is more of a suggestion. Grandma starts washing the few dishes that are in her sink. She washes everything right after she eats, dries them, and puts them away. "You know your momma is doing the best *she* can, right? Now, I'm not saying it's your fault her best not good enough, but, well, it is her best." Grandma turns the water off, takes her dish towel and begins drying a plate. "Love don't come natural to everybody. Love is something you've got to practice in order to get good at." She puts the plate in the cabinet and finishes drying the silverware.

"You want to get good at loving? You've got to be patient with your momma, be kind toward your momma. You've got to forgive your momma. Even if she don't ask for no forgiving. That's love."

I don't respond. I know Grandma is right, and besides I know better than to talk back or act like I'm not agreeing with her. I wait a little while and then strike up another conversation, hoping to focus on something other than me and my mom. "What are your plans for the day?" I ask.

"I was just straightening up a bit here before I head down to the lounge to work on my puzzle. I've started a new one. Finished that other one you and I were working on a while ago."

This is Grandma's way of telling me I need to come by more often.

"I'll help today," I tell her. While she finishes up in the kitchen, I scoot to the edge of the sofa and read the open Bible that is on the coffee table. At the homes of some of my friends, I've seen Bibles open to the middle of the book so that both sides are even. I've also seen it open to the same page every time, a favorite scripture or something. But not Grandma's Bible. Grandma's Bible is always turned to a different page when I come over because she actually reads it, actually has her own personal devotion right here in her living room. She fusses at my mom and aunts for not going to church anymore, reminding them that they were raised going to church every Sunday, that Sunday is the Lord's day, not a free day to lounge around the house, have brunch, and hang out. I never go to church—only a few times with Grandma when I was younger. So now, every time I come over, I make sure I at least read the scripture she has on display. I call it my three-minute church service. Sometimes, we discuss the scripture I've read, but most times, Grandma just lets me be, lets me take in the words for myself.

Today, the scripture is turned to James 2. She's high-lighted verses 14 through 18.

What good is it, my brothers and sisters, if someone claims to have faith but has no deeds? Can such faith save them? Suppose a brother or a sister is without clothes and daily food. If one of you says to them, "Go in peace; keep warm and well fed," but does nothing about their physical needs, what good is it? In the same way, faith by itself, if it is not accompanied by action, is dead. But someone will say, "You have faith; I have deeds." Show me your faith without deeds, and I will show you my faith by my deeds.

I read it twice, let the meaning sink in.

"All right, I'm all finished here," Grandma says.

Even though I just made myself comfortable, I get up from the sofa and put my shoes back on. We leave Grandma's apartment and make our way to the lounge, also known as the recreation room. The room is a long rectangular space with sofas and armchairs dividing the room so that on one side, people can sit and watch the big-screen television that is always turned up so loud it's a wonder people outside can't hear the reruns of *Matlock*. The other side of the room has bookshelves with books, board games, and magazines. There are square tables with mismatched chairs and a card table against the wall where pieces of Grandma's puzzle are neatly laid out.

A man with a short salt-and-pepper beard is sitting at Grandma's table. Next to him is an oversized mason jar full of iced cold tea sitting on the table, staining the wood with its condensation. "Well, what you say? Is this Miss Nala?" He smiles and wobbles up to shake my hand. "Oh, don't look worried—I'm no psychic; your grandma just talks about you all the time. She's shown me pictures," he says. "You can call me JT."

"Hi, JT. Yes, I'm Nala."

JT sits down and brushes his wrinkled fingers over the puzzle pieces. "You come to help us put this thing together? Me and your grandma been plugging away at it all week."

Grandma sits down. "It's Annie Lee's *The Beginning of Jazz*." She holds up the box. "Just beautiful, isn't it? Over a thousand pieces, though, so it's taking a while."

I join them at the table and start working.

Grandma clears her throat and says, "JT, what you got there in that jar? *Diet* iced tea, I hope."

"No, ma'am. Now I done told you, a man my age ought to be able to eat and drink whatever he wants whenever he wants—"

"Your doctor said—"

"I don't care nothing about what them doctors are saying. I ain't never smoked, ain't never had not one ounce of alcohol in this body. If sweet tea take me out, then so be it." JT takes a long sip of his tea.

Grandma shakes her head. "All right, okay."

I laugh because this sounds like an exchange Grandma would have with my mom or with Aunt Ebony. Not necessarily about how much sugar they are consuming, but she'd be fussing about something. She is the queen at fussing at people—making sure they are eating enough of the right thing, that they are wearing the appropriate clothes based on the weather, that they are getting enough sleep.

This is how Grandma loves.

JT takes another drink from his glass and starts spreading out puzzle pieces. He snaps them in place, and we work silently until my phone buzzes and sends trembles across the table.

It's Tye.

I send it to voice mail.

I can feel Grandma looking at me.

The phone buzzes again, alerting me that Tye has left a voice message.

I turn the phone over and keep working on the puzzle.

"Well, someone sure did put a smile on your face," Grandma says. "Who is he?"

"What makes you think it was a guy calling?"

"Only young puppy love brings about that kind of grin. You can't even contain yourself." Grandma smiles, and then she looks at JT and says, "I know that smile. I know that feeling."

JT smiles at her, and I realize that maybe JT is not just a neighbor who hangs out in the lounge with Grandma. Maybe he is more.

"So, who is he?" Grandma asks again.

"His name is Tye. I just met him, he's not . . . we're not—"

"He makes you smile. That's a good start," Grandma says. She goes on fitting puzzle pieces together.

My phone buzzes again. This time it's a text message from Tye wanting to know what time I get off work. Just seeing the words "off work" fills me with guilt. I type back in an hour and turn my phone over.

Soon, Grandma's friends join us. Ms. Norma—who is always knitting something, Ms. Louise—who dresses up every day like she's going someplace fancy, and Ms. Mabel—who uses a scooter and is known to not-so-accidently run into people she's annoyed with. They don't help with the puzzle; they just sit and watch and gossip.

Ms. Norma starts it off. "You all hear that racket last night with Catherine's grandchildren running around here like they ain't got no home training?" She is sitting in the rocking chair, swaying back and forth, pulling her needle in and out of the yarn.

Ms. Mabel nods her head. "Girl, yes. I don't know why them kids are allowed to run around the halls."

The women laugh.

"No home training at all," Ms. Mabel says. "Look at the wall right there. Catherine's grandson marked it all up with a crayon. They just going to leave it there?"

"Maybe they think it's art," Ms. Louise says, laughing.

Grandma says, "Hmm. Would be nice to actually have some art on these walls. Everything here is so bland." She points to the wall on the other side of the room. It is a

52

dingy white with only one medium-sized framed photo of a field of flowers centered in the middle. "That's a sad, sad wall," she says.

Just then, JT clears his throat. "Um, Nala, I think maybe someone is here for you." He points toward the door.

I turn around. "Tye?"

"Ah, the boy who makes her smile," Grandma says.

"Tye, what . . . why . . . what are you doing here?"

"I thought we could hang out this evening. You said you got off work in an hour."

"Work?" Grandma asks.

I quickly walk Tye out into the hallway before Grandma asks any more questions. I didn't realize how much time went by. "Um, I'm glad you stopped by," I say.

"I hope I'm not going to get you in trouble with your boss. I guess I should have just waited outside."

"No, no—it's fine. Um, give me a minute to get my stuff. Wait out here."

When I go back into the recreation room, Grandma and her friends have moved on to talking about how hot it is this summer, hotter than they ever remember New York being in July, and JT is saying, "Maybe this climate change thing is real."

I wait for a moment before interrupting. "Excuse me, Grandma, I, um, I have to go. I forgot that I have a, I have a thing to go to." A thing? Clearly I need to get better at lying.

Grandma stands. "A thing, huh? Well, it was nice to get some time with you." We hug and she walks me to the door.

"You don't have to see me out. I'm okay."

"Oh, no, I want to meet this *thing* of yours," Grandma says, smiling brighter than Harlem's sun. All the women laugh.

JT adds, "And let me know if I need to have any words with this *thing*. You know, man-to-man," he says as he winks at me.

I walk into the hallway with Grandma. Tye is leaning against the wall scrolling on his phone. He puts it away once he sees us. "Oh, hello. Hi," he says.

"This is my grandmother, Ms. June," I tell him.

Tye reaches out his right hand. They shake. "Nice to meet you, Ms. June. I'm Tye."

"All right, well, we're going to go." I try to keep this short so Tye doesn't start asking about my job that doesn't exist. We say our goodbyes, and I think I've made it out without any awkwardness but just as we get to the door, Tye turns around and says, "Maybe I'll come back and volunteer here too. Must be nice having Nala working here." Grandma looks confused. I don't give her time to try to make sense of what Tye just said. I quickly wave good-bye and walk away as fast as I can.

"You like Ethiopian food?" Tye asks. We're walking along 135th, just past the YMCA at Adam Clayton Powell.

"I've never had it," I admit.

"Oh, we've got to go. It's, like, one of my favorite kinds of food." Tye keeps walking toward Frederick Douglass. Before we get to the end of the block, he stops and says, "This is one of my favorite spots. My uncle takes me here a lot." He opens the door to Abyssinia Ethiopian Restaurant, and I walk in. The lights are low, and there aren't that many people inside. A brown woman greets us and takes us to a table at the window.

I look over the menu and ask, "What are you getting?" Thinking I'll follow his lead. He says, "The veggie platter. You want to share?"

"Oh, sure," I say.

Is this a date?

Tye closes his menu. "So the thing about Ethiopian food is that you eat it with your hands. No forks. You okay with that?"

Absolutely not, I think. "Sure," I say. I excuse myself to the bathroom so I can wash my hands. I get a glimpse of myself in the mirror, and I look away before I really have to see myself. *What am I doing?*

By the time I am back at the table, the server has come and taken our order. I can tell because the menus are gone and we both have full glasses of water. I take a sip. "So, all I know about you is that you're active in Inspire Harlem and you enjoy volunteering and doing work in the community. What else is there to know about Tye Brown?"

"I think that about sums me up. That's who I am."

"That can't be true. You don't have any hobbies? No family? What do you care about?" I ask. "Tell me something about you that I don't know."

"I don't know what to say—I, let's see, I care about leaving this world in better shape than it is for us. My uncle always tells me that's my sole responsibility. He's always saying some quote about service being the rent we pay for our room here on earth."

"Are you two close?" I ask.

"Yeah. My uncle is kind of like my dad." Tye clears his throat, and for the first time, he looks away from me.

"I understand. My aunt is like my mom. I live with her."

"Imani's mom?"

"Yeah."

I can tell Tye wants to ask me a question, that he wants to know more about me and my mom and why I don't live with her, but I think he knows that if he asks about me, I'll ask about his situation, so he just takes a sip of water, looks out the window. And I'm glad because I don't want to talk about my mom today.

Our food comes on the biggest platter I've ever seen. When the server sets it on the table, I immediately smell ginger and garlic and spices I don't know the names of. Tye seems happy to change the subject. "Okay, here we go," he says, pointing to each section of the oversized plate. "These are vegetable sambusas," he says. "And this is cabbage . . . potatoes . . . collards . . . split peas . . . and chickpeas." Then he points to a spongy-looking bread and tells me, "This is injera. The best part of the meal." Tye shows me how to stuff the food into small pieces of the injera, and we start eating—me making a mess, him being neat and put together.

I don't ask any more questions about family, but I do go back to my question about what he likes to do. "So, when you're not hosting a talent show or planning community block parties, what is Tye Brown doing?"

He laughs. "I don't know. Reading, I guess. I like to read."

Reading? "So, what you're telling me is you don't have any fun, like, ever?"

"I have fun all the time. I like volunteering, and

reading is, I don't know—it's relaxing, and I learn a lot about other people—"

"Tye, you've got to start doing things that aren't about speaking up for anyone, aren't about learning about someone else's culture—just fun. It's summer. You can't waste it being so serious all the time." I take a big bite of food. So far, the greens and chickpeas are my favorite. Maybe being vegetarian isn't so bad. I swallow, then say, "I'm going to teach you how to have fun."

"And what do you want me to teach you?" Tye asks.

He looks me in the eyes, and I think he might be putting a spell on me. I can't talk or move. I want to lean forward, kiss him, and tell him something provocative about all the things he can teach me, but instead, I take a long drink of water.

"What, you don't think I can teach you anything?"

I try to think of something clever to say. I flirt back. "Well, what do you want to teach me?"

"Do you have any questions about Inspire Harlem?"

Oh, wait. He's being literal. He really wants to teach me something.

"I thought maybe you might want to continue the conversation we were having the other night when we were all talking about music and the messages we get from media. Seems like you had a lot more to say."

This is not a date.

"I, um, no—I don't have anything else to say about that."

"Oh, because, you know, if you ever, um . . . if you ever want to talk about stuff or ask me questions or just, I don't know, tell me what's on your—"

"Are you trying to recruit me for Inspire Harlem? Is that why you're spending time with me?"

"What? No. No—why would you . . . no." Tye is sweating a little, so he wipes his brow with his napkin. "I guess I'm not good at this. What I'm trying to say is, I want to get to know you. I just—I don't know, you seem like you have a lot you want to say but you don't say it. The other night, I really wanted to hear your thoughts. You can, um, if you want, you can talk to me." Then, Tye starts laughing. "I guess I could have just said that instead of trying to be cool with the whole *what can I teach you* thing."

"Um, yeah."

We are laughing, and my nerves settle a bit. And I realize Tye is just as nervous as I am.

Maybe this is a date.

"I want to get to know you too," I tell him.

"Good. I'm glad to hear that." He picks up his glass and offers a toast. "Here's to a new friendship."

Friendship?

Then this is not a date.

I slowly lift my glass, clink it against his. To friendship . . . for now. But by the end of summer, I'll figure out a way to get him to want more, to want me.

We start eating again, and Tye says, "The other day Ms. Lori had us working on our college applications. There's a series of workshops Inspire Harlem is offering— financial aid, writing the personal essay . . . have you started yet?"

"Um, yeah. I'm trying to get early decision too."

"Let me know if you ever want to work on your essay together. Maybe we can write together and swap to give each other feedback."

"Sure," I say. I'm not as far along as I should be, so it might take a while. And by not as far along, I mean I haven't started. I have no idea what college I want to go to. I don't even know what I want to do, who I want to be. I get good grades and all, but I think I should do a community college first, then a university. I don't know if Aunt Ebony is going to go for that. One of the agreements I committed to when I moved in was to keep my grades up and excel in school. Going to college was implied.

Both Aunt Ebony and Aunt Liz have master's degrees. My mom doesn't even have her bachelor's. No one in the family has ever outright said it to me, but the unspoken hope is that I don't turn out like my mom. That alone is one reason that makes me want to go. I might not enroll to a big fancy school right away, but I'm going to one day. Even my mom wouldn't have it any other way.

Our conversation goes on and on. The server has taken our plate, given us hand wipes, and refilled our glasses so many times, I've lost count. Tye is full of questions, asking me what movie I last saw, what my favorite thing to do on a Saturday is. We talk about our childhoods—favorite cartoons we watched, games we used to play, and then Tye says, "Okay, so Nala Robertson loved *Rugrats* and *Dora the Explorer*, used to be the double dutch queen of her block, loves the singer Blue, is a vegetarian, and works as a program coordinator at Sugar Hill Senior Living."

"Yep. That pretty much sums me up." Well, kind of.

"Any pet peeves?" Tye asks. "I've got to know what not to do."

I laugh. "Um, I don't know. Smacking," I say. "I hate when people chew with their mouths open, you know? It just really annoys me."

"Um, is this your way of telling me I was chewing with my mouth open?"

"Not at all. You have perfect manners." Perfect everything. "What about you?" I ask. "What are your pet peeves?"

"People who randomly sing out loud."

I laugh. "Really? What do you have against music?" I tease.

"I just—come on! No one wants to hear an off-tune version of a stranger's favorite song."

"But what if they can sing?"

"Nope. I don't want to hear it. I don't even want to hear music through someone's headphones. If a person's music is so loud that I can hear it, that's a problem. It's so annoying."

"Got it," I say. "I will never burst out in song when I am with you. And I will keep all music I am listening to, to myself. Anything else I should know about you?"

"Liars," Tye says. "I can't stand it when people lie to me."

And this is when I remember who I really am.

"So," Tye says. "About this fun you are going to teach me to have . . . where to next?"

5

I tell Tye to meet me at Riverbank in two hours. That's enough time for me to get ready—to change out of my regular, I-didn't-know-I-was-going-to-see-a-fine-boy-today clothes into something more suitable for a date. Riverbank overlooks the Hudson River and has an Olympic-sized pool, a wading pool, tennis courts, basketball courts, and an eight-lane track with a field that is sometimes for football, sometimes for soccer. But to be honest, I don't really care about all of that. I come for the skating rink. Now that it's summer, the rink has ended its ice skating hours and is strictly for roller skating. Tonight is Teen Skate Night, where the lights are dark and everything glows bright and fluorescent and the DJ plays all the best songs, one song leaning into the next like falling dominoes.

I open my closet, stand in front of it, and try to find an

outfit that's perfect for both roller skating and turning a guy-friend into a boyfriend. I decide to keep it simple and change into my cute, fitted jeans (taking off the I'm-just-going-to-see-Grandma jeans) and I look for a top. Everything I have is cute—I'd even say fly. But Tye seems like the kind of guy who likes a more casual look. I mean, just about everyone in Inspire Harlem wears graphic tees with some kind of message and I don't have any. I go into Imani's closet. I slide her hanging shirts, looking for one that's close enough to my style but still says I'm socially conscious. The first three graphic tees are of faces of women I don't even know, so I pass on those. And then there are two that are just a little too intense for me. But then I see one that's a perfect fit. A black shirt with white lettering that has a list of four names.

Marcus.

Medgar.

Malcolm.

Martin.

I text Imani and ask her if I can wear it. I know she'll say yes, but I always ask first when I borrow something from her. While I wait for her to answer, I do my makeup, put on my oversized gold hoop earrings and bangle bracelets. Now, all I have to do is figure out what to do with my hair. Is there such a thing as the perfect hairstyle to get a guy to like you? I doubt it. I go with the Inspire Harlem style and decide to wear a head wrap. Like Toya's. I've never worn one actually, but it'll be good to have one on tonight in case I sweat out my hair while showing off my skating moves.

Imani is always tying her hair up in a scarf or wearing a wrap, but it just isn't my style. I rummage through the wicker basket that sits on her dresser. It's stuffed with fabric. Every color combination and patterned design you can imagine, she has it. I pull out one that is a mix of blues, yellows, and reds. I go back to my room and begin wrapping my hair. I check my phone to see if she's responded to my text, then add **and one of your head wraps too?**

I take the shirt and fabric to my room. I go ahead and put the shirt on and then pull my hair up into a bun so I can do the wrap.

It's not working.

The fabric is too loose, and the knot at the front keeps coming undone.

I try again.

It's not working.

I'm going for the Black-girl-natural-chic look, and this is not it. I pick up my phone, google *how to tie a head wrap*. This makes me wish I had paid more attention when Mom tried to teach me. There are too many videos to choose from. I click on the second one since it has the most views. The woman in the video does three different looks, and all of them look so stylish and cute on her, all of them seem so easy to do. But every time I try, I fail.

I'm going to be late.

"Uh, you need some help?" Imani's home. I didn't even hear her come up the stairs. She walks over to me, takes the fabric out of my hands, and folds half of it into a triangle. How did she know to do that? The tutorial didn't say to do that.

"This is too big to use without folding it. You gotta fold it if you want this look." She points to herself, because of course she has her hair wrapped and she looks like she could model her whole outfit. "Sit here." She points to the chair at my desk and starts twisting and wrapping the fabric, pulling it real tight, then twisting it into a knot.

"Your hair is too slippery. You're going to need some bobby pins." Imani walks over to her room and comes right back with a few bobby pins hanging out of her mouth like fangs. "This is why I keep telling you that you need to stop straightening your hair. It can't even keep fabric on . . . no kink to hold on to." And then she realizes I am wearing her shirt and she says, "Wait, what is all this for anyway? You don't even wear head wraps."

"I'm going roller skating tonight. Don't want to sweat my hair out."

"It's definitely going to sweat out under this," she says. She tucks the extra fabric and steps back so I can look in the mirror.

"It's okay if I sweat it out and it's covered. I just want to look the same way at the end of the night as I'll look when I show up."

Imani goes back to her room. Then, a whole ten minutes later she yells across the hall, "Oh, sorry. I'm just now seeing your text messages." And then, "Who are you going with?"

I don't know why I am hesitant to answer her. I stutter out Tye's name. And all of a sudden she is back in my room. "You're going out with Tye? Tye Brown?"

"We're not eloping. We're just going to Riverbank." I laugh, trying to make light of it.

"Who else is going?"

"It's Teen Skate Night. I don't know who will be there, but I'll be there and Tye will be there."

She looks at me with suspicion and then says, "Well, am I invited or is this a date?"

"It's not a date," I answer. Not tonight, but soon. I have a plan. "Tye and I are just getting to know each other," I tell Imani. "Just two friends hanging out. You can come."

"Okay," Imani says. "I'll let Toya and Lynn know, and I'll see if Asher, Sadie, and Jackson can come too."

Wait. What? I should have said this is a date. I definitely should have said this is a date.

"I'm going to text everyone, and we'll meet you and Tye up there," Imani says. And just like that, I am going on a group field trip with teens from Inspire Harlem.

Tye is waiting outside for me, looking out at the water. He doesn't know I am behind him, and I think maybe I should scare him, but then decide to gently touch his back. "Hey," I say.

"Oh, hi. You look nice. I like this." He touches my wrap, and I cringe a little because I am afraid the bobby pins will slip out. They don't, though. Imani gave me extra, extra reinforcement. "This place is amazing," Tye says.

"You've never been here?"

"Never."

"How is that possible?"

"I feel judged right now," Tye says.

We laugh and go inside.

It isn't too long before everyone else shows up. I see Imani and Asher first, then Sadie and Jackson. It feels like we're on a triple date, and I can't believe it's this easy to make my plan happen. We stand in line to get our skates, and that's when I hear them. Lynn and Toya. Their voices dragging out, "*Heeeeey.*"

So much for my triple date.

Toya looks different from the last time I saw her because her hair is all out, a big gorgeous mess all over her head. "Hey, Tye, you lookin' good with the fresh fade," Toya says. They hug, and when Tye lets go he says, "Yeah, a haircut was well overdue. Your hair looks nice too. It's beautiful."

He is right, her hair is beautiful, but I don't want him to be the one to tell her. That's ridiculous, I know. How can I be jealous over someone I just met? He's not my boyfriend. Yet.

Standing next to Toya with her beautiful hair, I am second-guessing everything about myself—what I'm wearing, saying, and if I'm dancing too hard to a *problematic* song. But then, I think *what do I have to prove to any of them?* and I take Tye by the hand and pull him out onto the rink. "Whoa, whoa . . . slow down. I haven't skated since I was ten years old. Give me a minute." He holds onto the wall and says, "All right, before we start, let's take a selfie. Gotta capture the *Before* just in case this ends badly." Tye laughs.

"Are you scared?"

"Me, scared? Never," he says, while nodding his head up and down saying yes. "Scared is a strong word. It's just, like I said, I haven't skated in a long, long time."

"You just have to get out there. It's like swimming and

riding a bike, right? Once you learn you always know how."
I don't know if this is really true, but he buys it. "Smile," I
say, and hold my phone up in the air at an angle to capture
both of us. We take a few and skate around the rink.

Tye is holding on to me so tight, so very tight. I keep
telling him, *you got this, you got this.* By the time we go
around once, he is steady and sure and now we are dancing
and gliding next to each other and he doesn't need to hold
on to me anymore but I want him to.

I don't know how long we've been here, but I have seen
people come and go, go and come. Tye asks, "You want
anything to eat?"

And oh my goodness, how did I forget that the best
part of Riverbank is the food? The hot dogs, the fat, salty
pretzels, the popcorn fresh and hot and buttery. "Yes," I
say. We go over to the side of the rink. "I'll get us something," Tye says. He walks to the food counter, and I join
Asher and Imani, who are sitting on a bench. I sit next to
Imani. The rink is covered but not indoor, so even though
I can't see the sky, I can see that Harlem is dark now; the
sun is gone and there is relief from today's heat.

Toya and Sadie come and sit next to me. Toya hasn't
said much to me, just a soft *hello* and an *excuse me, sorry*
when she bumped into me while we were skating. She
takes her skates off. "This is a workout," she says. "I'm
tired."

Imani laughs. "This was fun. Can't believe we haven't come here before."

But we have. Imani and I came here all the time with my mom and her mom when we were little. But then I realize I am not a part of the *we* Imani is talking about.

Toya says, "Too bad we didn't think to bring the flyers for our community block party."

"Oh, you're right," Imani says. "There's at least one hundred teens here. Perfect place to spread the word."

Sadie doesn't give me a look, like she normally would, but she doesn't say anything either, so at least I know she disagrees with them.

I stand and lean against the edge of the rink. "Maybe it's good that you didn't—I mean, you know, it's okay to take a night off so you can just have fun," I say. Why can't I keep my mouth shut? They are clearly not talking to me. I am not a part of their *we*.

Tye walks over to us, drinks, popcorn, and pretzels in hand. Jackson and Asher are with him, carrying their own snacks. "What are you all talking about?" Tye asks.

Toya says, "Just talking about how this is such a missed opportunity. We could have brought flyers to promote Inspire Harlem."

Tye looks around and takes in all the people, all the bodies falling and whizzing by. "Oh, you're right. I didn't think of that."

Um, yeah—you didn't think of it because you were focused on spending time with *me*. They aren't even supposed to be here.

"Well, Nala thinks that's a dumb idea." Toya points at me. Imani gives her a look like she's saying, *don't start.*

"I didn't say it was a dumb idea. I said it's okay to take a break. That's all I said." I look at Imani and Sadie for backup. They know I didn't call anyone's idea dumb.

Sadie says, "Yeah, it's probably good that we didn't bring promotional material. If someone handed me a flyer promoting something right now, I'd probably throw it away."

There's back-and-forth about what I did and didn't say, and then, maybe in an attempt to make things better or to bring the peace, Tye says, "I get Nala's point. It's like Ms. Lori always says, self-care is important. When you're trying to birth a revolution, you still have to take care of yourself."

"So spending time with me is your self-care project?" I ask. "And here I thought you wanted to get to know me." I say this in front of everyone even though I don't mean to. And since when is their mission to birth a revolution. And what does that even mean, really?

The DJ announces last call. One more song and the rink will be closing. I get up. "I'm going to go back out there and skate." I leave Imani, Asher, Sadie, Jackson, Lynn, and Toya, with her beautiful hair, standing next to Tye who is holding the food he bought for us, probably wondering what is wrong with me and why the sudden mood change.

I don't know who he gives the food to, but soon enough he is cruising beside me. "You left me," he says.

"Last song," I say.

Tye skates with me, close. Our arms brushing against each other, and I almost fall, so I grab him, hold on to him until I am stable. "I got you," Tye says. "I got you." We circle the rink, and I can't let it go, I have to ask, "So roller skating is how you practice self-care?" I ask. Attitude in full effect.

"That came out totally wrong. I was just trying to get Toya to see your side," Tye says.

"I don't have a side," I tell him. And then, "Everything can't be about Inspire Harlem. I just wanted us to spend time together. I'm on *our* side."

I want him to be a part of my *we*.

6

All night long I think about the last song Tye and I skated to. I can't sleep because my mind is replaying moments of our day together: how our hands touched when we both dipped our fingers into the collards, how he wrapped his arm around my waist while we swayed side to side on our roller skates.

And then I remember Toya's hair. Her beautiful, natural, not-straightened hair. The kind of hair that has body and volume and bounce. Her hair is big, and it makes a statement when she walks into a room.

Tye called Toya's hair beautiful.

I want him to call my hair beautiful.

I go back into my bedroom, sit at my desk, and open my laptop to search for tutorials on how to get a twist out with straightened hair. From what I've watched so far, the hard part will be getting my ends to curl and crinkle. I've flat ironed it so long that my natural kink is kind of non-existent. The third video I watch shows how to put rods at the ends to make my hair curl. I've seen those rods in the bathroom on Imani's shelves. I watch the whole video twice so I memorize the steps, and then I look through Imani's hair products and get all the supplies I need.

The first thing I need to do is wash my hair. I pull up my Blue playlist on my phone to listen to while I'm in the shower. Not too loud, because I don't want to wake Imani up—although she could sleep through a hurricane. I am thinking about how full and luscious my hair is going to be and how the next time I see Tye he is going to look at me and say, *Your hair is beautiful, you are beautiful.*

When I am finished, I part my hair into four sections and follow the steps the girl in the video did. I know I don't have the best record with following YouTube tutorials, but it doesn't hurt to try. I follow all the instructions, adding styling foam and moisturizer, two-strand twisting sections of my hair into chunky twists, and then drying it a little with a blow-dryer, not letting it completely dry but getting just a little of the wetness out.

The noise from the dryer drowns out the music, and I hardly hear Imani knocking on the door. I turn the blow-dryer off. "Yes?"

"I need to use the bathroom. What are you doing?"

I open the door.

Imani looks at me with a mix of confusion and irritation. "You're doing your hair at three in the morning?"

"What? It's three o'clock?"

Imani yawns and stands with her hand on her hip waiting for me to leave.

I unplug the blow-dryer and go to my room. I'll clean up the bathroom in the morning. I've got to go to bed.

I don't even remember falling asleep. I just know that when I get up the next morning, the sky seems wide awake, like the sun has been out for a while. I look at the clock on my nightstand. It's already noon. I guess staying up so late had its effect on me.

The first thing I do is slowly take the rods out so I can see how my hair turned out. I expect to have thick black twists even more stunning than Toya's because my hair is longer and thicker.

But no.

As I undo my twists, gently taking out the curling rods, I see that my hair looks much shorter and doesn't look like a kinky fro at all. My hair shrank like clothes do if they've been left in the dryer too long, and I look like I have an old-school jheri curl. I tug on one of the curls, pulling it down. It reaches my shoulder, but as soon as I let go, it boings back up. I look like I am in kindergarten getting ready for Sunday church service with Grandma. Or like I am getting ready to be a bride's flower girl.

Toya looks older and sexy with her hair out.

This is an epic fail.

I run downstairs to see if Aunt Ebony has any advice on what to do, and as soon as I get to the middle of the stairway, I hear voices. And it's not Aunt Ebony or Uncle Randy. I hear Imani and Sadie and Jackson and Toya. And Tye. What are they doing here?

It is too late to turn around. Tye sees me first. He is sitting next to Toya, whose hair is still big and luscious, and everything opposite of my shriveled curls. I cannot believe that Tye Brown is actually in my house and here I am looking like a Shirley Temple wannabe.

Sadie is the first to say something. "Are you okay?" she asks. And I can see it in her eyes. What she is really asking is, *what did you do to your hair?*

I can't move or say anything. I just stand there on the steps looking at all of them and they are all looking at me. They are polite enough not to burst out into laughter, but the looks of shock on their faces is enough to make me run back to my room, except I can't get my legs to move.

Imani walks over to me. "Hey, Nala. Uh, we're having an Inspire Harlem meeting today. Planning the community block party."

"Oh, um, hi, everyone. Sorry . . . sorry to interrupt. Imani, is Aunt Ebony here?"

"No, she went to lunch with Aunt Liz."

"Oh, I—I wanted her to help me . . . with my hair."

When I say this, Sadie rushes over to the stairs like a superhero. "I'll be back," she says to the group. And she grabs my hands and walks upstairs with me.

When we get to my room, I close the door and really I just want to break down and cry. Tye Brown is in my house, and I look a mess. And it's not just my hair. I have on sweatpants and a raggedy tank top. Finally, I find my words. "I want to go natural," I tell Sadie. "And clearly it's not a good look on me."

Sadie is trying not to laugh, but I know she wants to. "It's—it's not that bad."

I just look at her.

"Okay, it's pretty bad. Um, why don't you let me braid it."

"I haven't had braids since I was in elementary school. I like my hair to be straight—maybe I'll just get a weave."

"Just trust me. I can do them a little bigger than medium and you can still style them. They won't be too stiff or heavy, I promise. You like the way I did Imani's hair, right?"

"Yeah, okay. Will you come to the store with me so I know what to get?"

"Of course. I can do it right after this meeting is over. Until then, just wear a wrap."

"I don't know how to tie a wrap."

"What do you mean, you don't—"

"Sadie, can you just do it for me, please?"

"I'll show you how," she says. And she picks up the fabric that I wore last night. "Okay, so first—you need to fold it like this . . . ," and Sadie teaches me how to do a head wrap in three different ways, and I think she should do a tutorial for YouTube because she's taught me how to do it and that is no small feat.

"You're missing your planning meeting," I say.

Sadie shrugs. "They'll be fine," she says. She sits on my bed. "So, since when does Nala Robertson want to go natural? Imani finally convinced you, huh?"

"Just wanted to try something new."

"For who?" Sadie asks.

All I can do is smile.

"Oh my goodness! For who?"

"No one," I say. "You know I'm always switching it up."

"Nala—"

"Just—what type of hair do I need to buy for you to braid my hair?"

Before Sadie can answer, Imani is at the foot of the steps calling her. "We're voting on something, and we need you to break this tie."

Sadie sighs. "To be continued," she says to me. And then she mouths, "Is it Tye?" and smiles.

I take a shower and put on some real clothes and go back downstairs ready to see Tye and redeem myself from the fashion fail that happened earlier, but when I go into the living room, he is not there. Everyone is gone except for Sadie and Imani. I go into the kitchen to grab a granola bar. "Your meeting is over?"

"Yep," Imani says. She is putting away the leftover snacks. Sadie is loading the used dishes in the dishwasher.

"Sadie is going to braid my hair tonight. You want to come? Maybe we can start our Netflix binge-a-thon."

"I can't. I have plans with Toya."

"More Inspire Harlem planning?"

"I hope not," Sadie says. "Two meetings in one day?"

"No, it's not for Inspire Harlem. We're just going to hang at her place. Probably watch a movie or something," Imani says.

"Well, it's not going to be one of the movies *we* planned on watching, is it?"

"Of course not, Nala. Why would I do that?"

"Why would you rather hang out with Toya than me and Sadie?"

"So now I can only spend time with you two?"

Sadie goes to the fridge and takes out a can of seltzer water. This house is her house. She opens the can. "Please don't put me in the middle of this."

I go in the fridge and grab a can of seltzer too. "I mean, the plan for this summer was for us to spend time together."

"Whose plan?" Imani asks. And the way she says it is like she's saying that being around me is the last thing she wants to do. Before I can even respond she takes it back. "Sorry, I didn't mean it like that—I just, sometimes I want—"

"What? You want what?"

"Nothing. Never mind." Imani puts away the last of the snacks and starts walking back to the living room. "Why don't we do movie night tomorrow night." She takes out her phone, then says, "Oh, wait. Tomorrow won't work. I forgot. Asher and I have plans."

"Okay," I say, trying not to sound too disappointed.

"We'll find time," Imani promises. "We've got all summer."

I know summer vacation just started, but still. Me accomplishing everything on my Summer To Do List is getting off to a shaky start. So far the only thing I've accomplished is finding a new hairstyle. And that wasn't even on purpose. Who knew finding time and finding love would be so hard?

1

4 THINGS I MISS ABOUT IMANI

1. The times we'd text each other full conversations
   even though we were just a room away.

2. The times Imani would wake up in the middle of
   the night and stand at my bedroom door,
   whispering, *You awake? You awake?* until
   she woke me, how she'd come into my room
   and we'd stay up talking all night long.

3. The times we'd make french toast on
   Saturday mornings and watch classic cartoons
   till noon and promise each other no matter
   how old we get we'll always make time for
   The Flintstones.

4. The times we'd do our best to control our laughter at the dinner table, at church, at school, at any time when we are supposed to be serious and something funny happens. All the times she laughed when I laughed, cried when I cried.

Imani disappears to her room, then comes back down and says, "So, I'm going with you when you get your hair braided."

I grab her and hug her and tell her thank you over and over—half playful, half serious.

She just shakes her head at me. "When are we leaving?"

"Ready when you two are," Sadie says.

The three of us go to a beauty supply store on 125th to buy the hair.

"Let's stop here first, though," Sadie says. She stops in front of a corner store. "I need some chips in my life."

"I need a beef patty and some coco bread," I say.

"Me too." Imani opens the door, and we all file in.

We each go straight to the food we want. Sadie gets two small bags of chips and orders two patties—one beef, one chicken. No coco bread. "Not all of this is for right now," she tells us.

"Even if it was, this is a judgment-free zone," Imani says.

Imani and I order our beef patties and coco bread. As soon as we leave, I go into the bag and start eating. I sink my teeth into the golden dough. It is thick and flaky, and the savory filling has the perfect amount of spice. All this deliciousness is sandwiched between the sweet coco bread, making this the best decision of the day. My taste buds are so happy right now.

We finish our food before entering the beauty supply store. The first thing I notice when I walk in is the Korean man sitting up high in a space that looks over us all. He is not smiling or frowning, just a plain-faced man watching shoppers sort through hair oils, shampoos, barrettes, blow-dryers, and combs. At the front of the store there are shelves of nail polish against the wall on the right. The colors are stacked in order of light to dark shades; some of the bottled liquid looks so similar, I have to look up close to see the different tint.

"Hair is in the back," Sadie says. She walks down the aisle of oils and shampoos. There are so many to choose from, and it seems like every shampoo and conditioner is mixed with something: shea butter, coconut oil, olive oil, argan oil. Aunt Ebony always laughs at us, saying she can't believe that we'd spend so much money on something that she can make at home.

When we get to the back, Sadie walks up to the counter and dings the bell. "I hope Ji Son is here." As soon as she says it, a woman comes out and smiles when she sees Sadie.

"Hello, my friend," Ji Son says. "How can I help you today?"

"Do you carry something similar to this?" Sadie holds her phone out, zooming in on a photo.

"Yes, yes. Right over here." Ji Son walks us over to the section where packs of hair are sold.

"Perfect," Sadie says. She browses through the options of color, holds a pack up to me, and says, "Yeah, I think you're a 1B." She grabs packets of hair, passing them to me and Imani so we can carry them.

"What about adding some color?" I ask.

"Oh yeah—you'd look good in any of these." Sadie points to the shades of brown. I choose a color that's close to what I wanted to do if I dyed my hair.

"Or, you can be bold and do this," Imani says. She is holding up one pack of purple and one pack of blue. She is laughing because she knows I would never do that.

Sadie, on the other hand, takes the packets from her and considers them. "These are actually nice colors. They'd work for highlights."

It makes sense that Sadie would want me to add color. She changes her hairstyle every few weeks—braids, twists,

Afro—and she dyes it or adds extensions in color, blond, burgundy, dark green.

Imani and I follow Sadie to the register. A woman is standing there cursing out the clerk because she can't return her items. "Store credit only," the woman behind the counter keeps repeating while pointing to the sign. After the manager comes out and calms the customer, I pay for the hair and the three of us leave.

Once we are at Sadie's, I take my head wrap off and sit down in a folding chair that isn't all too comfortable, but at least the seat is padded. Sadie begins to braid my hair, strand by strand, as we watch the first movie. She braids pretty fast, but still, it's going to take a while, so we'll probably get through two and a half movies—depending on how many breaks we take.

Sadie braids and we watch the first movie—pausing it once to take a bathroom break. When the movie is over, we stop so I can stretch my legs and so Sadie can rest her fingers. "Want to listen to music?" Sadie asks. She puts her music on shuffle so we are listening to all kinds of songs bouncing from genre to genre.

"Have you heard Blue's album?" I ask.

"Who is Blue?"

Imani laughs. "A new singer that Nala is obsessed with. She plays her every morning. Loud."

"I thought you liked Blue?" I say.

"I do," Imani says. "I like her. You love her."

"She's right," I admit. "I guess I'm a little obsessed, but she's so good."

"All right, all right, I'm sold," Sadie says. "Let's listen to her."

I sync my phone to Sadie's speaker. It's hard to keep still because Blue's music makes you want to dance. When we get to the end of the playlist, Sadie says, "Let's listen to that again."

"See? Good, right?" I tell her.

Imani rolls her eyes. "Are we really going to listen to the whole thing again?"

I push play.

We listen to the playlist one more time, and then we start the next movie. I sit back down in the chair so Sadie can finish my hair. Just as the opening credits roll, my phone buzzes. It's Tye: **Sorry I wasn't able to say bye to you after our meeting. I had to rush out. What are you doing tomorrow?**

I type a response: **Whatever you want me to do.**

No, that is way too forward.

I delete that and type again: **Why? What's up?**

Hmm. Sounds too harsh. Truth is, I promised Grandma that I'd come over and help her on her puzzle.

I write another text: **I have to go to work.**

Tye texts me right back and says: **Can we hang out after you get off work?**

Well, it's good to know my jheri curl didn't scare him away.

"Nala, who are you talking to?" Imani says. "You're not even paying attention to the movie."

I feel Sadie looking over my shoulder. "Probably texting the same guy she's getting all cute for."

"Um, I'm always cute, thank you, and there is no guy." I am laughing when I say this. And inside I am wondering if I should tell them about my crush on Tye.

"Wait, there's a guy?" Imani pauses the movie.

"Why do you sound surprised?" I ask.

"I—just, I didn't know."

"There's nothing to know . . . yet."

Sadie screams, "Yet? I knew it! See, told you, Imani."

"Um, you're in my ear," I remind her.

"Okay, focus. Who is he?" Imani crosses her legs on the sofa and gets comfortable like she is getting ready for a long story.

It feels like old times. Here we are hanging out and just talking about our lives. We haven't done this in months. This is exactly what I wanted summer to be. I don't know why I am hesitating to tell them I have feelings for Tye. We usually tell each other everything. "Okay," I say. "Don't make a big deal about this. We are not dating. I repeat. We. Are. Not. Dating. But I do kind of, sort of like Tye, and I think he kind of, sort of likes me."

There, I said it. I feel relieved actually.

Sadie shouts—in my ear—"I knew it. I knew."

Imani scoots to the edge of the sofa. "Tye Brown?"

"Um, do we know any other Tye?" I smile when I say this, but when I look at Imani, I realize her question wasn't for clarification—it is the kind of question that asks, *really?* Imani's face is all frowned up. "Why are you looking at me like that?" I ask.

"You don't seem like his type."

"Well, thanks for the vote of confidence, Imani."

"To be fair, he doesn't seem like your type either. You two are opposites."

Sadie says, "Well, they say opposites attract."

Imani leans back again, relaxes her face. "Right. Yeah—I mean, it's just a little surprising." Then she says, "I actually thought he liked Toya."

"Why would you say that?" I lean forward, and Sadie taps me on my shoulder, moving me back to the spot she needs me in as she braids my hair.

"What? I'm just saying—him and Toya seem to be good friends, and I thought maybe there was something there. Toya is into community organizing, and so is Tye, Toya is a vegetarian, and so is Tye. Toya—"

"Okay, Imani. I get it. I am not the recycling, Heal-the-World-Make-It-a-Better-Place social justice warrior like Toya. But you act like there's nothing about me Tye could like."

"I'm not saying that."

"She definitely didn't say that," Sadie says.

Imani gets up and goes into the kitchen to get more soda. "Look, Toya is my friend. And she really likes him."

"I'm your cousin." Your cousin-sister-friend to be exact. "And I like him too. And he's giving me vibes like the feeling is mutual," I say. I don't even know if it's true, but I need to say it, want to believe it.

"That's fine," Imani says. "I wasn't saying he shouldn't; I just said it was surprising."

I shouldn't have said anything.

Sadie's fingers dance with my hair, twirling and twisting. "But wait—are you two together or—"

"We're just friends, and I don't want to talk about it anymore. Can you turn the movie back on?"

Imani picks up the control, turns the movie on. She mumbles a *sorry*. But I don't acknowledge it. I just try to focus on the movie. But I can't.

You don't seem like his type rings in my head over and over. And of course, the reason why I'm so irritated is because Imani is right. She knows the real me, and she knows the real Toya. And the real Tye. And so what she's saying is, Tye wouldn't fall in love with *the real* me and having a new hairstyle isn't going to change that.

Imani pauses the movie again and says, "And speaking of friends who are more than friends. Sadie, what's up with you and Jackson?"

"Nothing. We really are friends. I know that's hard to believe, but for real. We're more like brother-sister."

"You've never kissed?" I ask.

"Nope."

"You've never thought about it?" Imani asks.

"Nope."

At the same time Imani and I say, "I don't believe you."

And we all start laughing.

Sadie says, "You know it really is possible for a guy and a girl to just be friends. I love him. But it's not like that. He's a good friend to me. And our parents have known each other all our lives. Our families are just close. I promise. I have nothing to hide. If I liked him, I'd tell you."

We let it go, watch the movie. When Sadie finishes my hair she wiggles her fingers, shaking out the cramps in her hands. Then, she picks up a mirror. "You like?"

"I love," I say.

Imani agrees. "That style looks good on you."

We experiment for a while on different hairstyles I can do, but for the rest of the night, I just wear the braids down.

When Imani and I get home, Aunt Ebony says, "Wow, you look so elegant with your hair like that. It's beautiful."

My hair is beautiful.

Well, according to Aunt Ebony. I wonder what Tye will say. I'm going to see him tomorrow, and I will look much better than I did this morning. I wonder what kind of response Tye will give me. There are so many ways people react to a Black girl changing up her hairstyle. Of course, there's the most ridiculous *can I touch it?* questions from white people, then there's the *how long did it take?* question from people who know better than to ask if they can touch it but are still so curious. There are the Black girls who have been wanting the style or just had the style and want to talk to you about it to compare notes on the experience. And then the people who totally ignore you, act like your hair has always been that way—which means either they hate the new style and would rather not say anything or they really like it but don't want to say it (out of fear or jealousy). Of course, the best response is a simple *I like your hair.* Why is that response the hardest?

Before I go to bed, I stand in the mirror, play around with the different styles Sadie and Imani showed me. I think about Tye and wonder if he's standing in the mirror thinking about what I'll think of his hair . . . probably not.

10 BLACK GIRL HAIRSTYLES THAT LOOK GOOD ON ME

1. Box Braids
2. Marley Twists
3. Sister Locs
4. Micro Braids
5. Two-Strand Twists
6. Goddess Locs
7. Bantu Knots
8. Halo Braid
9. Flat Ironed, Bone Straight
10. Any way I like it

8

BLUE PLAYLIST, TRACK 5

big & brown & beautiful

Chorus
if beauty is in the eye of the beholder
then look at yourself, take in your whole body
if beauty is in the eye of the beholder
then look at yourself, take in your whole body

Verse 1
and what the mirror whispers is:
girl you are exquisite
every strand of hair on your head is accounted for
you are that rare find, that one-of-a-kind
and no one—no one—is a better *you*

see how big and brown and beautiful you are
see how big and brown and beautiful you are

Verse 2
and what the mirror whispers is:
you standing here a somebody, a whole body
big and brown
and full lips and wide hips
and unmanicured and untucked
and unbothered
and all right
you alright, girl

Chorus
if beauty is in the eye of the beholder
then look at yourself, take in your whole body
if beauty is in the eye of the beholder
then look at yourself, take in your whole body

Refrain
see how big and brown and beautiful you are
see how big and brown and beautiful you are

The next morning, I take my time getting out of bed and

getting ready for the day. This afternoon, I'm going to Grandma's because I promised I'd come over to work more on her puzzle. Harlem is wide awake. The streets are full of traffic, horns are blowing, and there are bumper-to-bumper standstills even on the side streets. There are boys shooting hoops at the basketball court at the end of the block, and the man who sells flowers from his van is setting up in his usual spot right across the street from the bus stop. I think maybe I'll take the bus, but instead I walk and stop at the bodega to get chips and something to drink. Grandma used to have the best snacks, but now that she's not eating much sugar or salt, there's nothing to raid in her cabinets.

When I get to Grandma's I go straight to her hangout spot. She is there with her crew, sitting at her table, like always.

"Hi, everyone."

"Well, good afternoon, Miss Nala," Ms. Norma says. "I sure do like your hair." Ms. Norma's voice is like the wind; it blows through the room, and suddenly the others start in with singsong compliments like chimes blowing in her breeze.

After they go on for a while, they all get back to talking about whatever it was they were discussing. Grandma doesn't join in their conversation. Instead, she turns to me and says, "How is everything?"

"Everything is fine," I say.

Grandma's eyebrows rise, and she whispers, "And how is your new friend?"

The women all start paying more attention to us.

"He's fine," I say. I try to sound neutral. No smile, just a straight answer. I sit down at the table across from Grandma and start helping out with the puzzle. There's been a lot more added since the last time I was here.

"And how is Imani? Can't even remember the last time I saw her."

"She's good," I say. "Busy with Inspire Harlem."

"Humph." Grandma snaps in a puzzle piece that completes the bottom right corner—a man sitting outside in a meadow playing his guitar, a rooster at his feet. "She's the busiest teenager I know."

Ms. Norma says, "Girl, it's not like it was when we were raising our children. These young folks have full itineraries. Places to be, people to see."

Ms. Louise nods. "You right about that. I haven't seen not one of my grandchildren in, well, what, two months. This is the generation of go, go, go."

Ms. Mabel adds her opinion. "Busy doing nothing, if you ask me."

I feel bad that they're all being so hard on Imani. I tell them, "Well, she's not doing nothing, she's actually doing a lot of good for the community. She's—"

"Oh, I didn't mean no harm, Nala. You don't have to explain." Ms. Norma's knitting hands are moving fast, and it amazes me to watch someone make something so precious without even looking. She clears her throat and tells me, "I know all about that program Imani is in. My granddaughter is in it too. I'd sure rather have her occupied with volunteering than out there in the streets causing trouble."

Grandma scatters the puzzle pieces trying to find the one she's looking for. "Nala, we're just saying that a person can be so busy trying to care for their community that they don't even have time to care for the people closest to them. That's all."

And then, as if we aren't having a serious conversation, Ms. Norma holds up the blanket she is knitting and asks, "What ya'll think of this? It's for my first great-grandbaby. They haven't picked a name yet, but we know it's a girl. My first great . . . ain't that something?"

We all ooh and aah at the blanket, and there is so much pride in Ms. Norma's eyes. And she's right—that is something, that her family is expanding and growing, that she has mothered generations.

I take my phone out and take a picture of Ms. Norma without her even noticing. There is something about the way that she is careful with it, like her actual great-granddaughter is already here in her hands.

"You over there being the paparazzi, Nala?" Grandma sees everything.

"Just taking a few photos, that's all," I say.

And of course it's Ms. Louise who says, "Well, let me know, chile." She straightens her clothes and poses. "I'm ready now."

And for the next ten minutes I have become a photographer doing a photo shoot at the Sugar Hill home for seniors.

"Now, send me those, okay?" Ms. Louise says.

Ms. Norma says, "Louise, you don't have a cell phone or email. How you think she's going to send 'em to you?"

Ms. Louise looks a little confused.

"I'll figure out how to get them to you," I say. I put my phone away.

Grandma and her friends bounce from topic to topic. In this past hour we've gone from talking about Imani and all of us young people to politics to the sale on bananas that the grocery store is having, and then Grandma brings up the wall again. It must really be annoying her for her to keep complaining about it. "What are we going to do about this sad, dingy, plain wall? Should we ask them to at least paint it a warm color?"

"It's not just the color, it's that only one little picture is there looking all lonely," Ms. Louise says, laughing. She is adorned in pearls today and a sleeveless navy blue sundress. Her nails look freshly manicured. Of course she wants it to be something other than plain.

"Once my great-granddaughter is born, maybe I'll hang a big photo of her on the wall. Make this into my extended living room," Ms. Norma says.

We all laugh.

Then, I get an idea. "You all should hang up photos in here. Like, make this wall a tribute to all the families represented in the building."

They all sit, quiet. Maybe my idea is horrible and they don't know how to tell me.

Grandma sits up straighter in her chair. "You know, Nala, that's something to think about."

Knowing Grandma is even a little interested in this makes me sit up too, makes me think maybe I really should start doing some service projects here at the residence since I keep telling Tye that's what I do. Maybe my lie could turn into the truth. "I can help," I say. "I can ask for permission and collect the photos and frame them."

"Well, I think you should," Grandma says. "I think you should."

I get excited about this. I want to do something special this summer. I mean, it's not as big or important as what Imani and Tye are doing, but adding some warmth to this room and making it welcoming, honoring the people who live here? That's something.

My phone buzzes. It's Tye asking what I'm doing. I type back, **Planning a photo legacy project for the Open Studio at Sugar Hill.** Okay, it's maybe a tiny—well, a big exaggeration, but typing it out makes me really want to do it now. For real.

A photo legacy project.

I might not be a serious community organizer or a change-the-world type of girl like Imani and Toya, but this I can do, this I want to do.

Tye replies to my text: **That sounds amazing.** And then: **I want to be a part of this. Let me know how I can help.**

I'm trying to think of a way to tell him that I don't need his help. I don't want to drag him into this fake-but-kind-of-real project. I text back: **Okay.**

After I leave Sugar Hill Senior Living, I walk over to 135th and Lenox and meet Tye at the halal food truck that parks right outside the Schomburg Center. When he sees me walking down the street, he smiles, and I don't care what Imani says, this smile is not a friend smile. He hugs me, tight, and when he lets go he says, "Every time I see you, your hair is different."

I laugh because if only he knew the story behind my hair.

"I like it," he says. "You're so beautiful."

"Thanks," I tell him. I'm beautiful to Tye. I let the words sink in.

"Do you know what you want?" Tye asks. We're up next. He pulls out his wallet.

"Um, whatever you're getting," I say.

He steps up to the truck and orders. "I'll have two falafel gyros, please."

"Oh, and a bottled water," I say.

Tye looks at me. "Um, you don't have water?"

"No, I . . . no." I think he's going to lecture me like Imani does. She thinks I should carry around a reusable water bottle, but those things get heavy when they're filled with water and I don't want to lug that around in my bag all day. Plus, on every block you can get ice-cold water for a dollar and I always put the plastic bottle in the recycling bin, so what's the big deal?

Tye orders the water without saying anything, but I can tell he is bothered. Once our order is called, Tye says, "Where to?"

"Let's just walk and see," I say.

We walk slow because we are eating and talking, making our way down 135th toward St. Nicholas Park. We're not saying a whole lot, mostly talking about how good our gyros are and how we should have got an order of fries to share. Once we get to the park, we climb the stairs and I hope I am not out of all the breath I have by the time we reach the top. We find a bench to sit on, and now that I am finished with my food, I am thirsty but I feel awkward bringing out my bottled water. I do it anyway because it is too hot out here and after walking up the steps, my throat is dry. I drink my water, trying not to guzzle it down like I really want to.

Tye says, "I'm so glad we're doing this. I wanted to talk more about your photo legacy project."

"Is that all you want to talk about?" I say that with an attitude. I can't help it. But I did not come out here to see Tye today to only talk about old people and pictures.

"Well, I don't only want to talk about that, but—"

"Tye, what is this? What are we doing? Is there a *we*?"

Tye looks at me, smiles. "Do you want there to be a we?"

"I do, honestly, but I don't know how you feel. And I don't know how you feel about Toya."

"Toya?" Tye's eyebrows frown. "What does she have to do with any of this?"

"It's obvious that she likes you. Do you have feelings for her too?"

"I don't think Toya likes me, and I definitely don't like her. Not like that. I mean, we're just friends."

"Yeah, but you said we were just friends." We even toasted to it.

"Oh, but no—when I said you were my friend, I meant, you know, like . . . well, my friend that hopefully becomes more than that."

"That's not what you said."

"That's what I meant." Tye takes my hand. "I don't like Toya. Toya likes Toya. A lot."

I laugh. Tye laughs too.

"Well, I just want to make sure. I needed to know. I mean, you two have a lot in common."

"So do we," Tye says. "I love that you volunteer at Sugar Hill Senior Living; you're focused and know what you want to do as far as college. Oh, and you and I like the same kind of food."

Maybe Imani was right. Tye likes the fake me, not the real me.

I tell Tye, "I want us to get to know each other. Like, actually talk about more than Inspire Harlem or Sugar Hill Senior Living."

"Well, tell me something I don't know about you."

You don't know anything, honestly. "Um . . ." This is harder than I thought it would be.

"Okay, well, I know you and Imani are cousins. Tell me about your family—your parents."

"There's not much to know," I say. "My dad lives in Jamaica, so I don't see him too much. My mom? Well, we do better when we don't live together. I love her, but she's not good at being a mother." I don't know if that sounded mean, so I just turn the question to him. "What about you? Are you close to your parents?"

"My mom. Yes. She's my everything. My dad—not so much. Now we're good, but when I was younger, it was rough. My parents divorced when I was eight. Back then, my dad was not good at being a father at all. Or a husband. But now, he's remarried and he's a better man." Tye sounds sad when he says this, and then he says, "I'm proud of him for getting his life together, but I hate that he couldn't do it for my mom. He has a whole other family. They get the best version of him."

We stand and start walking through the park. There are families out sitting on blankets, a cyclist riding his bike, couples strolling hand in hand, and down the path I see a little girl chasing bubbles and popping them with her hands as the woman with her blows gently through a wand.

Tye keeps talking, and I'm so glad I am finally getting to know him and not just what he does for Inspire Harlem. "My dad lives in Connecticut and has a whole new family— two other children with his new wife. My uncle kind of stepped in and helped my mom. He's like my dad. So I get what you mean about not being close to your mom and having a stronger relationship with your aunt."

I notice that Tye said "new wife" and not "stepmom."

"My dad and I would probably get along better if he didn't lie so much."

"What do you mean?"

"He just doesn't keep his word. He's always making plans with me and then canceling them at the last minute." Tye shakes his head, lets out a long sigh. "I can't stand when people don't follow through. Make a plan, stick to it. Say what you mean and mean what you say."

9

It's the Fourth of July, and the whole family is gathering at Aunt Liz's. Her rooftop is the perfect place to view fireworks. Every time I come over to Aunt Liz's I see the kind of future I want for myself. She's a regular kind of fancy, nothing too over the top, but she is not simple by any means. Today, she has catered a feast. Jerk wings, pork ribs, curry shrimp skewers, rice and peas, mac and cheese, Jamaican festival—the best fried dumplings in the world—fried plantains, and serrano lime slaw. And the dessert table is full too. I'm already eyeing out my three favorites: rum cake, gizzada, and sweet potato pudding. Before we begin eating, we dig into the platter of mango, pineapple, and strawberries.

Aunt Ebony thinks having all this food catered is the most ridiculous thing. "You know, Randy could have grilled the meats, Liz. And I could've made side dishes.

You didn't have to do all this." And then later, "What do I owe you?"

"You don't owe me anything," Aunt Liz says.

A few people have started their fireworks even though it's not dark yet. With the view from Aunt Liz's rooftop, we don't need to have our own fireworks. Soon, we'll be able to see the colors burst against the night sky.

The elevator opens, and out comes my mom and Asher. "Look who I found in the lobby," Mom says. She walks over to the table and looks everything over, talking loud and oohing and aahing about all the food Aunt Liz ordered. Mom's extra-long nails are painted a bold yellow. Her hair is wavy today, hanging to the middle of her back. And I will absolutely be asking her for those sandals she's wearing. The heel is perfect, and that shade of brown goes with everything. I think about how Mom used to always tell me she didn't have money for this and that but always—and I mean always—she knew how to put an outfit together. She always looks like she has money even though she doesn't. Mom says hello to everyone and then comes over to the table and kisses me on my cheek. "How's your summer going?" she asks.

"Good."

"Well, you've got to give me more than that. What are you up to this summer?"

"Just, I don't know. I'm not up to anything. Whatever comes up."

Mom says, "And what about you, Imani?"

Imani tells her about the million and one things she's doing with Inspire Harlem.

Mom turns to me again and asks, "Why aren't you in that program? You don't need to be wasting your summer."

I stuff my mouth with a chunk of pineapple to keep myself from saying something disrespectful. That feeling of being happy to see my mom dissolves. She is who she is, always. No matter what, she finds a way to pick at me. Usually we last at least thirty minutes without an argument, but today she's in a mood.

Aunt Ebony comes to my rescue, saying, "Did you all know Nala had perfect attendance and a 3.5 GPA this past school year?"

"This your way of showing off that she's doing better with you than with me?" Mom rolls her eyes and goes to sit down at one of the tables covered by an umbrella.

"All right," Aunt Liz says. "Um, let's . . . let's eat."

"Yes, let's," Mom says.

Then Aunt Liz opens the cooler and says, "Oh no, I forgot to get ice."

This means Imani and I will be walking to the bodega on the corner to get two bags of ice for the cooler.

I am the first one at the elevator.

Asher comes with us. We head down on the elevator, and when we get outside it's like we've entered a whole different world. Up top, things were serene, but down here the noise is piercing, especially the man with the bullhorn who is reading from a book, loud and passionate like a preacher on Sunday morning, "What, to the American slave, is your 4th of July? I answer . . . the gross injustice and cruelty to which he is the constant victim. To him, your celebration is a sham; your boasted liberty, an unholy license; your national greatness, swelling vanity . . . There is not a nation on the earth guilty of practices more shocking and bloody than are the people of the United States, at this very hour . . ."

We step into the store. "I guess not everyone's having a happy Fourth of July," I say.

Imani laughs, but then says, "He's reading Frederick Douglass's speech, 'What to the Slave Is the Fourth of July?' He gave it on July 5, 1852."

How does she know this?

We take the ice bags from the freezer, pay for them, and walk out. Imani continues, "Could be a speech given today, don't you think?"

I say yes. Asher does too.

Imani smiles at the man with the bullhorn, and he nods toward us, a nod that says, *We're in this together,* even though we don't know each other, even though I'm not sure what *this* is.

His voice trails behind us the rest of our walk. "Allow me to say . . . I do not despair of this country . . . I, therefore, leave off where I began, with hope . . . a change has now come over the affairs of mankind . . ."

We get back to Aunt Liz's and step onto the elevator. "That was intense," I say.

Imani presses the button that has the letter *R* on it. We head back up to the rooftop. "I'm glad someone's out there speaking the truth," she says.

"Right?" Asher says. "I mean, I'm down for some good food, but he's right, what are we *really* celebrating?"

I think about it—what are we celebrating? Then I say, "I think the fact that you can ask that question out loud with no fear . . . that's one thing we're celebrating." I really don't want to get political, especially not with Imani and Asher, so then I add, "To me, it's just an excuse to hang out with family and eat the best barbeque ever. Most holidays are about family time to me."

The elevator dings.

We get off, walk over to the cooler, and suffocate the drinks with ice, making sure the bottles and cans are covered.

Aunt Liz announces, "Everyone, come fix your plates

and eat." She makes sure we all have our plates before she gets any food. If hosting parties and family gatherings is a talent, she has it. "Randy, you want to pray over the food?" she asks.

I put my fork down because I was definitely about to dig in, not even thinking about blessing the food.

Uncle Randy calls out to get everyone's attention. "Let's say grace." Then, "Dear God, we thank you for our freedom, we thank you for this family, we thank you for this food. Bless it and us. Amen."

Even after I'm pretty sure every one of us has gone back for a second plate, there is still food left. Asher is sticking close to Imani like Velcro. I sit with them and talk a while before we get up for dessert.

"Did you eat enough, sweetheart?" Grandma asks me.

"Yes, Grandma. I'm fine."

"And you're good, Asher? You drinking enough water? It's hot out here."

"Got my water right here," Asher answers. He holds up his own reusable water bottle and clinks it against Imani's bottle as if he's giving a cheers.

Aunt Liz says, "Imani, before you get to fussing at me, please know I've had a big case of water that I want to get rid of. After this, I won't be buying any more plastic-bottled water."

"I wasn't even going to say anything this time," Imani says. "I wasn't going to mention that most plastic water bottles end up in landfills, and as they decompose, they give off harmful toxins into the environment. Nope, wasn't going to say anything about that." Imani smiles and takes a long drink from her metal water bottle.

Aunt Liz says, "I know, I know. This is my last case. I promise."

The sky is black and ready. Colors fill the air, and we are all pointing, saying *wow!* and *look!* I take a few photos with my phone, but they don't capture how stunning everything is. Having my phone in my hand makes me want to call Tye. I wonder what he is doing, if he is looking up at the sky seeing the same constellation. I hesitate, then send a text: **thinking of you.** I have been dishonest about a lot of things with him, but this is true. He is on my mind, and I am thinking and thinking if we even have a chance. I am thinking how if he were here tonight, if he had walked to the store with me, he probably would have known that man was reading a speech by Frederick Douglass, he would be critiquing the fact that we celebrate this holiday, asking if any of us are really free.

As we watch the sky sparkle Aunt Liz says to me and Imani, "I'll be traveling a lot this summer, so I want to spend as much quality time with you as possible." She takes a bite of rum cake. "I'm hosting a brunch on Saturday. You two are welcome to come."

I tell Aunt Liz I can make it, but Imani says, "I might be able to stop by." Like she is some important executive who has a ton of business meetings or something.

"Stop by?" Aunt Liz puts her hands on her hip. "What, you and Asher got a date or something?"

"Inspire Harlem stuff," Asher says. Like he wants to make it clear that he'd never pull her away from the family.

Imani adds, "Inspire Harlem has programming on Saturdays, so that's why I can't make it."

"Well, I guess that's a good excuse," Aunt Liz says.

Aunt Ebony joins in. "But it won't be the same without you. If your event ends early you've got to come by."

Imani nods. "Okay," she says, but I know her and I know that tone. I know when she means something and when she doesn't.

The night ends with Imani in Asher's arms, standing in a corner by themselves watching the sky glow. I am standing with my mom, splitting the last seltzer with her. "You know, when you were a little girl, you were afraid of fireworks," she tells me. We gaze out at the sky, the explosions of color coming nonstop. "You'd cry and cry at the sound of fireworks. You would have been terrified at something like this. Hated everything about the Fourth of July." Mom laughs at the memory. "Funny how people change."

Mom is talking about me; I'm thinking about Imani.

4 THINGS I'VE NEVER TOLD MY MOM

1. That the week before I moved out, I heard Mom crying in the middle of the night. A sobbing cry, a flood of despair. A cry that lasted and lasted until her tears rocked her to sleep.

2. That the night before I moved out, I heard Mom crying on the phone telling someone (Grandma? Aunt Ebony? Aunt Liz? one of her boyfriends?) that money was tight, that a two-bedroom apartment cost too much, that things would be easier if she didn't have to take care of me.

3. That the day I moved out, I started that argument on purpose because I knew she'd never kick me out but that I needed to go.

4. That every day since that day, I have missed her. That it's not that I don't love her, I just need more than she can give.

❧ 10 ❧

Today, Aunt Liz is having her brunch. She's invited a few of her close friends, and two of her clients are here too. Both of them are up-and-coming singers. We've all gathered on the rooftop. Well, not all of us. Imani is not here. And neither is my mom. Even Grandma is here, and I know she is not pleased that her daughter and granddaughter are not coming.

Aunt Liz has catered the brunch. The spread looks just as fancy as the one on the Fourth of July, but there's not as much food. Just ackee and saltfish, fried bammy, and callaloo.

"I could have made breakfast, Liz." Aunt Ebony says.

They have this conversation every single time we gather here.

Aunt Liz says, "This is supposed to be a chill day. I didn't want anyone to have to do anything." She fills her glass with cranberry juice and takes a sip. "So, Imani is really not coming, huh?"

Aunt Ebony sighs and sits down at a table. "Not this time."

I wonder if there will ever be a time when Imani puts her family first and tells Ms. Lori she can't make the meeting, or the event, or the special whatever because she is spending time with her family.

"Aw, I really wanted to spend some quality time with her," Aunt Liz says.

"Me too." Aunt Ebony shakes her head and repeats herself, "Me too."

Aunt Liz asks, "Nala, is your mom coming?"

"I don't know."

She looks at her watch, says, "Well, okay, then, let's go ahead and eat."

Aunt Ebony stands and walks over to the food table to make Grandma's plate so that Grandma doesn't have to get up.

Before I fix my plate I stand at the balcony and look down. Being up this high makes everything below look like a miniature land of make-believe people walking their dogs, riding their bicycles.

"Come eat, Nala," Aunt Ebony says. "What are you over there thinking about?"

Grandma chuckles. "Her new *friend*, probably."

Here we go.

Aunt Liz says, "Do tell, do tell."

Aunt Ebony's eyebrows are perched high, and she is leaning forward, her whole body asking, "What?"

I just walk over to the table and fix my plate, not saying a word.

Aunt Liz clears her throat. "Come on, now, at least tell us his name."

I give in and smile. "His name is Tye."

"Good to know. I'll leave it at that . . . for now," Aunt Liz says. She can tell that I don't want to talk about it, and she never makes me talk when I don't want to. I don't know why I haven't talked with them about Tye. I think maybe it's because if I start bringing him around, he'll start getting to know the real me.

Grandma looks at Aunt Liz and says, "And what about you? Any new names we need to know about?"

"Mother, please."

Whenever Aunt Liz calls Grandma "Mother," it is not good.

"Please, what? I'm just asking a question. Would be nice to see you get married before I pass on."

"Really, Momma? Really?" Aunt Ebony steps in. She gives an apologetic look to Aunt Liz's company.

They all seem right at home and are enjoying the conversation.

Aunt Liz clears her throat. "Okay, here's the situation—when there's someone to tell you about, I will. Until then, you can assume that there are no good prospects."

"But aren't you at least going out on dates?" Grandma asks.

I'm glad she can be nosy and all up in Aunt Liz's business because I want to know too.

Aunt Liz says, "I recently met a guy online, and when we got together in person he was absolutely nothing like he presented himself to be in his profile. I mean, what, did he think I wouldn't notice? I don't understand why people lie to get someone's attention. Don't they know the truth will come out?" Aunt Liz starts laughing when she tells us how his pictures had to be at least five years younger and lots of pounds lighter and that he put "self-employed" when he should have put "unemployed." "Big difference," she says.

We all laugh, but inside, I feel a twinge of guilt wrapping around my heart. Grandma sips her orange juice and says, "Well, I guess I need to keep on praying, then. It would be nice have some new grandbabies around here."

Aunt Liz just shakes her head.

We eat, and then people group off in twos and threes and talk and mingle. Once the first person announces they are leaving and says goodbye, all of Aunt Liz's friends start making their way to the elevator but not before hugging us all and thanking Aunt Liz for hosting.

Now it is just family. Grandma, Aunt Ebony, Aunt Liz, and I go inside because now the afternoon sun is blazing. We stay at Aunt Liz's, talking all afternoon. Then, Aunt Ebony turns on the television and we watch a marathon of *Living Single*. Every time we say "Okay, last episode," we can't help ourselves and we watch the next one. Grandma has dozed off only twice. I'm impressed. Usually, the TV is watching her instead of the other way around. So many times when I'm at her apartment and we're watching television together, Grandma closes her eyes. I usually wait till I know for sure she is asleep and then I change the channel. No matter how quiet I am, Grandma jumps up out of her sleep and says, "I was watching that."

The sun has settled into the sky, and Aunt Liz orders pizza, and we feast because what we ate for brunch has worn off. I keep checking my phone to see if my mom or Imani has sent a text. Nothing.

Just as the theme song comes on for the next episode, my phone rings. I thought I had it on silent, but it's loud, and now everyone has turned to me like we're in a movie theater and I'm being a nuisance. It's Tye. I stand up and answer the phone, walking into Aunt Liz's bedroom.

I close the door. "Hello?"

"Hey. Want to join us for dessert?" Tye says. I love that we are familiar enough with each other that when he calls, he just jumps into the conversation.

"Like, right now?"

"Yeah. We just finished up with Inspire Harlem, and we're going to Sugar Hill Creamery. You should come."

I really want to say yes, but I can't just leave. "Thanks for inviting me, but it's kind of a family night," I tell him. Then, realizing who the *we* is that he's talking about, I ask, "Is Imani going with you?"

"Yeah. It was her idea."

"Oh." And I don't even need to ask who else is going. I know Asher is with her, and Sadie and Lynn are there and Toya with her beautiful hair.

"Next time," Tye says. "And it'll just be me and you."

"Okay."

"It's a date," he says.

I smile. "See you soon."

I stand in Aunt Liz's room for a moment. I need to swallow the tears that are trying to rise. I don't know why I am so emotional. Maybe it's because there used to be a time when Imani would have rushed home after an event to be with us, when she would have sent me a text to ask me to save her something to eat because she knows Aunt Liz goes all out for our gatherings. And while it feels good that I am on Tye's mind, that he wants to spend time with me, I wonder why Imani didn't invite me. She always invited me out when it was just her, Sadie, and Lynn. But now that Toya is around, I feel like I'm losing my cousin-sister-friend.

When I get back into the living room, I sit back down in my spot, at the right end of the sofa. I grab a throw pillow, hug it to my body.

Aunt Ebony turns to me and whispers, "What's wrong?"

"Nothing," I say. "Everything's fine."

"You sure?"

"I'm sure," I tell her. Even though I'm not sure about anything.

11

I heard Imani come in late last night. Like, later than Aunt Ebony allows, and I know there's no ice cream shop that stays open that late, so I wonder where she was. Probably with Asher. His mom doesn't have strict rules about curfew or friends coming over. He can come and go as he pleases with whoever he pleases. Imani is still sleeping. Her TV is on because she can't sleep without noise. I don't know how she does that. I need quiet when I sleep. I get up and get dressed, text Tye to see what he's up to today, and go downstairs. By the time I get to the kitchen, he has responded: *seeing you I hope.*

My smile overwhelms my face.

Uncle Randy comes in to refill his coffee. "Well, someone's happy this morning."

I put my phone in my pocket. "Good morning, Uncle Randy."

"You, ah, you got a minute?" he whispers.

I lower my voice too, even though I don't know why we're talking like this. "Yes."

"Okay, so your aunt went on a walk with Liz, so that's why I wanted to talk to you now while she's gone. Is Imani up yet?"

"She's still asleep."

"Okay, so one of us will have to fill her in," Uncle Randy says. He is still whispering and looking around the kitchen like at any minute he will get caught. "So, ah, your aunt's birthday is coming up—well, it's at the end of August, so we have a little bit of time—"

"It's just the first week of July. We have plenty of time," I tell him. He doesn't look too convinced, and then I remember that Uncle Randy is a pre-preplanner. He is the most organized person I know. I am surprised he doesn't already have it all worked out. I cut up an apple, eat a slice, and savor it. Aunt Ebony always buys Pink Lady apples, our favorite because of the sweetness.

Uncle Randy says, "I want to do something really special for her, but, well, after being with her for so long I think I've kind of run out of things to do." He rubs his head. "Now, you know she hates surprises, so that's out, and she's not too flashy, so nothing over the top."

"Right," I say. I take out my phone, open my Notes

app, and make a list as we come up with ideas. We start with gifts.

"What about a weekend away? You two could go to the Poconos. She'd like that," I say.

"Yeah, I was thinking Cape Cod, actually. Or maybe a spa day," Uncle Randy says. "But she always gets her nails done anyway, so is that special enough?"

"Well, it's special if she doesn't have to pay for it." I laugh. "And you could add some treatments to it—a massage or a pedicure. That might be nice."

Uncle Randy seems to like but not love this idea.

I type it into my notes anyway, and we think up a few more: brunch at Central Park's Boathouse restaurant, good seats to a Broadway play. "What about a candlelit dinner on Aunt Liz's rooftop? Just family and close friends?" I ask.

"Perfect. Yes, I'll ask Liz."

Imani yawns her way into the kitchen. "'Morning," she says.

"It's twelve thirty," Uncle Randy says. "Good afternoon." He kisses her on her forehead.

Imani squints at the clock. "I was out late last night with Inspire Harlem."

Eating ice cream, I think.

Not inviting me, I think.

"What are you two doing?" she asks.

Uncle Randy starts whispering again. I laugh a little and remind him that Aunt Ebony is not here, so he doesn't have to talk low. "We're planning something nice for your mom's birthday," Uncle Randy says.

I hold my phone up and show her the list.

"You two are planning Mom's birthday?"

"Well, we're just coming up with ideas right now," Uncle Randy says.

Imani opens the fridge, takes out the pineapple juice, and pours a glass. "Wow, you're just planning it all without me?"

"You were sleeping, Imani. Nala is just helping me think up ideas."

I set my phone down, sit at the table in the corner nook of the kitchen. "I was going to fill you in."

"Filling me in means you were going to already have a plan and just share that plan with me but not ask me to help come up with the plan."

"Well, it's not my fault you were out all night and couldn't wake up this morning," I say.

"Nala, I always help my dad organize something for my mom's birthday." Then she turns to Uncle Randy and asks, "Why would this year be any different?"

I eat the rest of my apple and put my plate in the dishwasher. I don't have time for Imani's attitude. "We literally just started talking about it." I pull up Imani's number on my phone and text her the list of notes. "There, you have the ideas now. You can take it from here." And then I add, "You are so sensitive. Always thinking someone is trying to leave you out. This isn't sixth grade." I try to say it with a smile, but I think it comes out as harsh as I actually feel it.

"Sixth grade?" Imani asks.

"You don't remember the epic Christmas-tree-decorating incident?"

Uncle Randy chuckles and walks away. "This is my cue to exit stage left." He walks out of the kitchen.

"Don't leave now, Dad," Imani says. The memory must've come back. "I know you all think I was over-reacting that night, but it really didn't seem fair that you all did the Christmas decorations without me."

Uncle Randy calls out from the living room. "You were sick. You had the flu and had finally fallen asleep. Your mom and I were not going to wake you." He's said this so many times.

"Well, I was only eleven and it felt like you all were being a family without me. It was *our* tradition."

And when she says *our* I realize for the first time that each time we retell this story it is not funny to Imani, it is not just about the time she had the flu and a fever and missed decorating the tree, missed baking peanut butter blossom cookies, missed making hot cocoa. For Imani, it is about the night her mom and dad took me in as their own daughter, the night when we bonded without her, the night I moved in. Stayed.

I always look back on that rainy day as the day everything changed in my life for the better. Me, dripping wet from the rain, showing up on the doorstep like a lost puppy. I never considered that maybe for Imani it was the beginning of her life changing in ways she didn't want. On my first night in her home, there I was joining in on a family tradition that wasn't my own. She cried when she woke up and saw the tree. I remember the look in her eyes when she asked, "But who did the angel?" and Uncle Randy told her I did. She couldn't even have any of the cookies because her stomach wouldn't hold water, so she just went to bed having to fall asleep to the laughter of her mom and dad and her cousin-sister-friend celebrating and welcoming in the holiday season without her.

Tye and I meet up at Sugar Hill Creamery. He is there before me and already has a booth for us, in the back. When I get to him he pulls me to him, holds me while he's talking to me. "You good?"

"I'm okay."

"Just okay?"

"Let's get ice cream," I say.

We walk to the counter and order. Tye, salted caramel. Me, strawberry chocolate chip. Tye pays, grabs napkins for both of us, and we walk back to the booth. One side has a bench connected to the wall, the other side chairs. He pulls a chair out for me, knowing that I'd be more comfortable sitting in the chair than crammed up in the booth. He is like that, knowing what I need when I don't even ask. Never making a big deal out of my size. As soon as we sit down, he says, "Okay, lay it on me. What's up?"

I can't believe this, but all the emotion I held in yesterday is still there. That's the thing about tears. If you don't cry them, they come out in other ways or just wait for another time. And here they are.

Tye reaches out for my hand. "What happened?"

"Nothing. I—nothing happened. And I think that's why I'm so emotional."

"What do you mean?"

"Nothing. Just . . . our ice cream is going to melt." I pick up my spoon, but Tye won't let it go.

He leaves his side of the booth and comes to sit next to me. "You can tell me anything."

And I believe him, so I tell him about the brunch and how Imani never came and my mom never came. How things are changing between me and Imani, how they are staying the same between me and my mom. How sometimes I feel like a burden to the people who are supposed to love me, the people who are supposed to be there, always, no matter what. "I don't want to talk about Imani behind her back. We're good. I know she loves me. It's just—things are different."

"You don't have to do that," Tye says.

"Do what?"

"Downplay how frustrated you are. Of course she loves you, but that's not the point. And that goes for your mom too." Tye squeezes my hand. "I know all about family drama. Believe me. I get it."

But it's not just the family drama. It's me not being fully honest with him. It's me not knowing Fredrick Douglass's Fourth of July speech, it's knowing that Imani would rather be anywhere but home with me, it's knowing that every time I spend time with Tye and get to know him better, I like him more and more and I don't know how to be the real me, or if he'd even like the real me. Yeah, these tears are about all of that.

We finish our ice cream, and then we just sit and talk since it's not too crowded and no one is waiting for a table. Tye stays next to me, and I love how he keeps my hand in his hand, how even when he is not saying words, he is telling me something.

12

I've seen Tye every day for two weeks. Besides having dessert at Sugar Hill Creamery, we've been to see two movies, took a walk along the High Line, and sometimes, we pick a neighborhood to explore. So far, we've roamed around Washington Heights, Union Square, and the West Village. Summer feels slow because the sun hangs on to the sky as long as it can, like it doesn't ever want to let go. And this is how I feel holding Tye's hand. I want him with me always. Tonight, we are sitting on a bench at the West Harlem Park Piers watching the Hudson River swallow the sun. It is cooling down now, and my legs have stopped throbbing from the walk we took to get here.

Tye leans back on the bench, says, "Tell me something about you that I don't know." This has become a thing now. Whenever we have run out of things to talk about or if there is an awkward silence, we ask this question.

It takes me a while, and then I say, "I don't have a favorite color."

"What do you mean, you don't have a favorite color? Everyone has a favorite color."

"Not me."

"Come on—"

"There are colors I like, but I don't have one color that I love or that I decorate my room with or wear a lot."

"I don't know anyone who doesn't have a favorite color," Tye says.

"Well, now you do. What's yours?" I ask.

"Tan."

"Tan? Be real, your favorite color is not tan."

"Are you judging me?"

"Yes, actually. I mean tan being your favorite color is worse than me not having one. Tan is so bland, so boring."

"Tan is not too bold or bright," Tye says. "And it matches everything. I like neutral colors," he tells me. "And I don't look at neutral colors as bland or boring. I think they're just laid back. Chill."

"Like you," I say.

He smiles.

"I'm serious. That's a perfect description of you. Laid back and chill. Gets along with everyone. That's what I like about you."

"I like that about you too," Tye says. "You're just—I love the way you make having fun a priority. Like, you are always thinking of someplace to go, something to see in the city. It's relaxing to hang out with you." Tye takes my hand, and how is it that one touch from him sends shock waves through every part of my body? "And I love how you love," he says.

"What do you mean by that?"

"You just—it's so clear how much you love your grandmother. How you started a whole volunteer program just to be closer to her, to make sure she had activities to do. That says a lot about you."

I let go of his hand. This would be the perfect time to come clean. To tell Tye that actually I love beef burgers and that this morning I had scrambled eggs with extra, extra bacon. This is the perfect time to tell him that my grandmother's facility is just her home, not a place where I work. We have only hung out for two weeks, with no kissing, no nothing that says we are something serious, so now would probably be the best time, the right time to tell him who I really am. Because the way he looks at me, the way we make it our business to talk to each other every day, see each other as often as we can . . . something more is coming. He's wanting to get closer and closer to me, and I want him to know exactly who he is getting close to. That's what I should do—tell him now. I take a deep breath, turn to him and start to talk, and instead of words coming out of my mouth, Tye's lips press into mine. And there is no talking, only kissing, and kissing and kissing.

Tye asks if I'm ready to leave.

"No, let's stay a little longer." I take a plastic water bottle out of my purse and drink, trying not to get too much lipstick on the bottle.

"Ms. Lori gave us a summer challenge not to drink out of plastic water bottles," he tells me.

He sounds like Imani right now, giving me a not-so-gentle hint that I am doing something wrong. I don't say anything.

"Uh, not that I'm telling you that you should take the challenge. I was just saying, I'm taking the challenge."

I don't say anything. I drink the last of my water. Make sure every drop is gone. There's a garbage can not too far away, so I get up and walk over to it. As soon as I get to the can, I catch myself. I don't throw it away. Instead, I put it back in my purse, sit back down next to Tye. I'll wait till I find a recycling bin. That's the least I can do, I guess.

I have a feeling if I had thrown it away, there'd be a lecture, a look of disapproval.

We sit for a while longer looking out at the water. A few boats sway and rock on top of the waves. "Okay," Tye says. "Tell me something else I don't know about you."

"I can't think of anything."

"There have to be more things that I don't know about you."

"But I can't think of something I want to share right now." I could tell him that something he doesn't know about me is that I hate feeling judged, I hate feeling like I am not good enough. But who likes being judged? I mean, that should be obvious.

He looks at me. "Okay, I'll go." And then he leans back and says, "Remember when you asked me about my relationship with my father?"

"Yeah."

"I wasn't completely honest with you."

Tye wasn't completely honest? Maybe we all have secrets.

"I told you I love him, but sometimes, I—I kind of hate him too."

I take Tye's hand. There's nothing I can say right now. I just squeeze his hand, try to let him know that I understand.

"He's just . . . so I saw him yesterday. He was here for some business meeting or whatever, and it's not like he even planned to see me. It was so last minute. So unorganized. He only had like an hour because he had to get back to Connecticut. Couldn't miss his train." Tye is quiet for a while. There are so many questions I have for him. I want to know what he and his dad talked about, what he wished they'd talk about.

There are always the words we said and the words we wished we said when it comes to the people we love.

"I don't want to care, you know? But, like, he was sitting there bragging on his children, telling me how well they did this past school year, how good Nathan is in sports. And I'm sitting there like—what about me?" Tye stops talking when he says this, like he didn't mean to admit that last part. But it's too late to take the words back, so he keeps talking and I keep listening. "I don't mean to sound conceited or anything, but I mean, I'm handling my business, I'm doing the right thing. I'm making sure my mom is proud of me, that I get a scholarship to college so she doesn't have to stress about tuition. I'm out here doing all this Inspire Harlem stuff, and he sits there and talks about his five-year-old son playing Little League. Really?"

I can tell Tye has been holding this in since yesterday, that this is the first time he's let any of these words out. He takes a deep breath, says, "He's the one missing out, though. I try to remember that. At least that's what my mom says."

"My aunt says that too," I say. "All the time. She says my mom is missing out on my best years and that it's not my fault."

Tye squeezes my hand. I lay my head against his chest. He puts on an exaggerated game-show-host voice and says, "And that concludes our most depressing round of Tell Me Something I Don't Know about You." Then, in his real voice, "Sorry about that. I just needed to—"

"You never have to apologize for telling me how you feel."

Tye lifts our hands, kisses mine. "Your turn. Something funny, something—"

"Tye, it's okay. It's okay to sit here and be sad. I mean, you don't have to wallow in it all day, but you don't always have to look on the bright side of things. Sometimes, you have to acknowledge what's hurting you. How else will you ever heal?"

We sit and sit, letting the sadness sink in, holding each other and watching the boats sway and sway until the sun has vanished and the sky is a kaleidoscope of pink, purple, and orange. I take a few photos of the river and the sunset. Then, I pull Tye up, yanking his arms toward me. We turn around so that the sunset is our backdrop and take a picture. Just as I am taking the second one, Tye kisses me on my cheek. I take the photo. Tye says, "Send that to me."

"Okay." I crop the photo, center us a bit, and then send it in a text. I save the photo to my background so I can see it every time I pick up my phone.

We stand and start walking back through Harlem's streets. We pass Dinosaur Bar-B-Que, the Cotton Club, and continue home. The whir of the number one train above us flies through the sky like a rocket. The more we walk on 125th the more crowded it gets. We walk closer together as the sidewalks narrow.

"Tell me about the community block party," I say.

"So, you know how our tenets for Inspire Harlem are Remember Harlem, Honor Harlem, Critique Harlem, and Love Harlem?"

I nod.

"Well, this event is focusing on Love Harlem," Tye says. "The only thing Ms. Lori said is, we have to make the community aware of one social issue we care about." We stop at the corner until it's safe to cross and then keep walking. "We're focusing on loving the Earth."

I am just listening, waiting for Tye to get to the part where he talks about the block party, the fun stuff.

Tye continues. "There will be tents along the street with volunteers handing out flyers and brochures about ways to take care of the environment and how to become more engaged in the local community. We've invited a few experts to give talks and demonstrations throughout the day."

Finally, I have to ask. "But what about this is a *party*?"

Tye sighs. "I know. To be honest, I haven't figured it all out. And I need to because it's happening soon. My team is great, don't get me wrong—Imani, Toya, and Asher have taken care of all the technical, practical things we need for the day. The flyers are printed, the brochures are ordered. The vendors are booked. But yeah, we have some more thinking to do when it comes to the party aspect of things."

"What about getting a DJ? And maybe you can have a face painting station in case there are children. And a few stations where there are games or something—"

"Like trivia questions for a prize," Tye says.

"Yeah, you need some actual fun things for people to do or else they're just going to come get some food, maybe grab a flyer, and leave."

Tye squeezes my hand. "I should have had you on my team from day one."

We walk the last few blocks to my house, and soon we are standing at my stoop. We hug, and Tye doesn't let me out of his embrace. He whispers, "Can I kiss you again? Here?"

I answer with my lips, leaning myself into him, and we kiss, blocking out the city noise, not caring who is walking by. When I go inside, Imani is at the window not even trying to hide that she was watching us.

"You two been together all day?" Imani asks.

"Yes."

"You a couple now?"

"Yes."

Imani walks away from the window, goes into the kitchen, and looks through the fridge for something, maybe anything. "Wow. Tye is dating my cousin."

"Is that a problem?" I ask.

"Not at all," Imani says.

But I don't believe her.

13

The community block party is off to a great start. 135th Street is blocked off from Lenox to St. Nicholas. There's a big banner at both ends that says, Love Harlem. Volunteers are posted at both ends at the Inspire Harlem tents. Jackson and Asher are at Lenox Avenue to greet community members and hand out reusable water bottles and a tip sheet on recycling. Vendors line both sides of the street, and so far, my favorite is the woman selling jewelry that is made from recycled soda cans. Down the street at St. Nicholas, there's a resource tent. Lynn is there giving out a calendar of community events and a handout with local resources, like websites and numbers to hotlines, food banks, and shelters. An adult volunteer is there with voter registration forms and keeps telling people who walk by, "Show your love by voting—in every election. Every election is the big election." She sounds like an automated recording the way her voice stays the same every time she says it.

There are all kinds of food vendors and local businesses in between the two tents lining the street with their booths. The DJ is playing mostly songs Ms. Lori would approve of, but occasionally she throws in something all the young people want to hear.

I'm not even a part of Inspire Harlem, but here I am at the face painting station decorating kids' faces, transforming them into butterflies and superheroes. Tye asked me to help Sadie. She is painting a girl's face, making her into Shuri.

I have just finished a little girl's face who only wanted a heart on her cheek. I take a picture of her, and then I take a few of the full crowd, try to capture all that's happening. Sadie and I take a few selfies. Most of them come out horrible, but there are a few good ones that I think I'll keep.

The line ebbs and flows throughout the day. Every time we think we're done, more little ones show up. The line just grew, and I am trying to paint fast but not so fast that I make a mess on someone's face.

Tye comes by to check on us. "You good?" he asks.

"Thanks to Nala," Sadie says. "You see this line? No way I could do all these faces."

Toya walks over to our tent with her beautiful hair,

beautiful everything. She took her ordinary, boxy volunteer shirt and turned it into a cute summer crop top. She is with Imani, whose shirt is also cut up and remixed to look much cuter than it actually is. Toya gives us both a hug. "Hey, Nala. Didn't know you were coming."

She actually said my name this time.

"Yeah, Tye asked me to help. I wanted to support him."

Tye puts his arm around me. "She's the one who came up with the idea to get a DJ," he says. He goes on about the ways I helped brainstorm activities for the day. I like that he's bragging on me. Maybe I am good for him after all.

Toya forces a smile, says, "Nala, I keep telling you, you should join the group." Her mouth is telling me this, but her eyes tell me something different. "Enrollment doesn't open till fall, but until then you can be our *honorary* member."

Imani laughs. "Nala is not going to join Inspire Harlem. You might as well let that go."

As if Toya means it anyway.

Sadie says, "You should think about it, Nala. We'd see each other even more."

And even though Sadie is talking to me, Imani says, "Nala is just not into this. Not everybody is made for Inspire Harlem. Just leave her alone about it." Imani looks at me with a tender, cousin-sister-friend look, and I realize she thinks she's defending me. But really, I feel small.

I can't blame Imani for how things got this way between us. Our whole lives she has been told, *look out for your cousin . . . take care of her . . .* She was handed a role she didn't audition for. I can't think of a time when she wasn't there for me, showing me the way. Family legend is that she walked first and started trying to pull me up and teach me how. Even when she didn't know how to read, she'd hold a picture book in her tiny, chubby hands and read to me in her gibberish, holding the book out so I could see the illustrations. Imani is the one who taught me how to tie my shoes, how to double dutch—how to leap in without getting my thick legs caught in the rope. And then there were the lessons about our bodies, about crushes, about pulling all-nighters to study for the next day's test. Imani has always been a few steps ahead of me, always reaching back to take my hand, pull me forward with her.

Maybe it's time for both of us to let go. Walk on our own.

Finally, the line has ended and Ms. Lori tells us we can close up our station and visit the vendors before the program begins. Tye looks at his clipboard and walks away with Ms. Lori toward the stage.

Sadie and I pack everything up and step out from under the tent. This is when I realize how many people are here. And now, without the tent to cover me, I feel the hot sun on my skin. I mean, well, it's hot but it's not scorching like earlier this week, which is good. Today, there's even a slight breeze. I think this is why so many people are out. We've all been cooped up under air conditioning as much as possible. But not today.

"Let's start on this side and then walk back on the other side," Sadie says.

"I'm hungry," Toya says. "I'm going over to the food carts." She tries to get Imani to go with her, but Imani stays with me and Sadie.

Sadie leads the way down the left side of the street, me and Imani behind her like shadows, collecting handouts and free samples in our Inspire Harlem tote bags. The three of us start trying on the soda can jewelry, holding up one of the handheld mirrors to see ourselves. "What do you think of this?" Sadie asks. She has on big circular earrings that look like crushed black and red metal. They used to be a can of Cherry Coke. Imani and I answer at the same time—me saying I love them, Imani saying no. Sadie agrees with me. "I think I'm going to get them."

Sadie and I laugh, and then Imani gives in to a laugh too. And it feels like old times, when we would walk 125th Street and try on things and take them off, swapping them with one another, saying, *this would look better on you* or *let me try that on.* We keep walking, making our way down to see the rest of the vendors. It feels like we're breaking some kind of rule walking in the middle of the street. I've always loved street fairs; besides the funnel cakes and shopping, there's a vibe that makes me feel unrestricted, free.

After we get to the end, we make our way back to the main stage just before the program begins. Ms. Lori takes the stage first and says a few words—first thanking the sponsors of the event, and then she says, "Before we get back to the music, food, and activities, I'd love for you to hear from our young people today. They are the force behind planning this event, and they truly care about our community. I am so positive, so very sure that these young people will be leading the way in years to come. Please show them some *looove.*" Ms. Lori calls on the core planning team to say something at the microphone.

First Tye and Asher. Asher just waves to the crowd and lets Tye speak. Tye keeps it short, thanking everyone for coming out. Then Imani steps up and thanks Ms. Lori for her mentorship and then encourages people to take all this energy with them, back to their homes and work spaces. "Please take the time to read all the handouts you're getting today and challenge yourself to put some new things into practice," she says.

Toya is last. She takes the mic, and she talks longer

than any of them. "Dr. King said, 'It really boils down to this: that all life is interrelated.' This means, everything you do or don't do for the Earth impacts another person. This means it is important to not only take care of yourself, but to make sure your neighbor has what they need."

When she says this, there are a few people who snap in the air like they are at a poetry café. Some of the older people actually say *amen*. Toya continues . . . on and on and on. She quotes James Baldwin and Chimamanda Adichie and Fannie Lou Hamer and Shirley Chisholm. She is a book of quotes; everything out of her mouth makes the audience cheer or clap. I can see her one day preaching or lecturing and inspiring people to be more and do more than they ever thought possible.

I am irritated, inspired, and intimidated by Toya. Yeah, all three pretty equally. Not a good feeling.

Toya stands on the stage taking in all the applause and cheering, like she knows she deserves it. Then, she looks at me and smiles, real big. "Before we turn it back to the DJ, I just want to acknowledge our *honorary* Inspire Harlem member. She came out today just to help and volunteer even though she is not a part of the program. She even helped our team leader, Tye, with some of the ideas for today. Let's welcome Nala Robertson." She waves me to the stage.

I do not move. At all.

"Don't be shy," she says. "Come say a few words."

The audience is clapping and waiting and waiting. Tye takes my hand and walks me to the stage. My feet are disobeying my mind. All the good sense I have is saying, *do not go up there.* But somehow here I am, standing on a stage in front of hundreds of people. When Toya hands me the mic, she smiles at me and then cuts her eyes so fiercely that my soul bleeds.

My hand is shaking, and when I open my mouth, nothing comes out. Imani can't even look at me—she is literally holding on to Asher with her head buried in his chest. I clear my throat, try to speak.

Nothing.

Nala, get it together. Just thank everyone for being here. That's it. That's all I have to do. But Tye already did that, and besides, after a talk like Toya's I've got to say something powerful, something moving.

Quotes.

Toya's remarks were mostly other people's words—not her own. That's when people really got revved up. I think maybe the best speeches are when the speaker says the words other people have already spoken. I think and think of inspirational quotes I can recite. I stutter out the first thing that comes to mind. "Um . . . good afternoon. I, um,

I agree with everything that's already been said. It's, um . . . it's important to get involved in our community and to learn about what's happening around the world—especially, um, especially People of Color and especially girls, because, I mean—um, who runs the world? Girls!"

No one claps.

"That's, um, that's what Beyoncé says. Girls . . . run the world. But we can't run the world if we, um, if we destroy our world. So we have to take care of it, love the Earth, you know?"

Nothing from the audience. Just the sound of a siren moaning in the background and maybe laughter from some of the Inspire Harlem members. Even still, I can't stop myself. I just keep talking and talking and I don't even know what I am saying. It's as if every song I know just comes to mind and somehow ends up coming out of my mouth. "Because there's a lot happening in the world. You know? I'm sure you're all like me, looking at this world and seeing the effects of climate change, and, um, all the movements happening—Black Lives Matter, the Me Too movement, Say Her Name . . . and, um, you're all wondering, like Marvin Gaye—what's going on?"

No one claps or nods or snaps or says amen. Instead the opposite happens. People start heading back to the carts to get food, and some people walk away, like actually leave. But still, I keep talking. By the end, I've reverted to some cliché quote about dreams and change and trying your best. And then, finally, the DJ rescues me by cutting me off and saying, "Yes, yes, that's right. Come on and put your hands together for our young budding activist . . ." She plays a song I don't know that gets the crowd dancing.

I put the mic back on the stand and run off the stage—the opposite side of where Tye is standing. I don't say good-bye to him or anyone else. I walk home, fast as I can. As soon as I am in the house, Aunt Ebony asks, "How did it go?" but I don't answer her. I just run upstairs, go in my room, hide.

Imani doesn't care that I am already in bed when she gets home. She comes into my room without knocking and starts with, "What is going on with you? Like really—what was that today?"

"I don't feel like talking—"

"Oh, we are definitely talking. You are not going to embarrass me like that and then act like it's no big deal."

"Embarrass you? I embarrassed myself, Imani." I don't turn over to face her. I am still in my bed, lying on my side, back to the door.

"Well, I couldn't tell," Imani says. "I mean, you just kept going on and on. Were you trying to make fun of our program? Of Toya? Of all the hard work we do?"

I sit up, lean against my headboard. "No, I wasn't trying to make fun of Inspire Harlem. Everything isn't about you and Toya, you know." My room is dark, and I am surprised Imani doesn't turn the light on. But I am glad. Talking with her like this, not having to really see her, makes it easier. Right now we are just shadows, just ghosts of ourselves.

Imani sits at the foot of my bed. "You're changing."

"I thought you'd be happy. Haven't you always wanted me to be more socially conscious?"

"But not for a guy. You're just trying to impress Tye."

"And Toya was just trying to make a fool of me—which she clearly succeeded at. Are you going to talk with her too? Do you even care that she humiliated me by calling me up to the stage, knowing I am not a part of Inspire Harlem? I swear, you are loyal to everyone but your family."

"Are you serious right now?" Imani gets up from my bed. The mattress shifts, then settles again. "I share my mom and dad with you, and you think I'm not loyal to our family?" Imani walks to the door. She is crying, I think. It is too dark to see her sadness, but I hear her tears. She leaves my room. I get out of bed, follow her.

It is dark in the hallway too. Dark and familiar because I never turn the hall light on when I get up in the middle of the night to use the bathroom. "Imani, wait," I call into the night. "Today was all about loving the Earth and loving your neighbor. Well, what about loving your family?"

I think about what Grandma and her friends said about being so busy you can forget what's important. "You're out there doing all this work for the community so much you're not even here for the people who care about you. When is the last time you saw Grandma? Aunt Ebony and Uncle Randy hardly see you." I head back to my room, but before I go in, I turn and say, "I might not know all the social justice quotes and I might not be the world's greatest teen activist, but I am here for my family. And I'm proud of that."

Imani's door slams. I didn't even see her move.

3 QUOTES TO LIVE BY (AKA: THE QUOTES THAT HANG ON IMANI'S BEDROOM WALL THAT I SHOULD HAVE PAID MORE ATTENTION TO)

1. Choose people who will lift you up. Find people who will make you better. —Michelle Obama

2. Nobody's free until everybody's free. —Fannie Lou Hamer

3. Revolution is not a one-time event. —Audre Lorde

14

The next morning Aunt Ebony has made Uncle Randy's favorite breakfast—corned beef with onions and bell peppers and hash browns with a sunny-side-up egg on top. We hardly ever have breakfast together. During the school year we are all rushing out and grabbing the quickest thing available, which is usually a granola bar. But today, Aunt Ebony has called us downstairs to eat, not caring if we were awake or not, if we are hungry or not.

When we get to the table, I am sure Uncle Randy and Aunt Ebony feel the tension between me and Imani. I try not to make it too obvious, but I can't pretend that I am still not frustrated. For the first few minutes at the table, the only sound is the clanking of forks against plates and the occasional slurp of pineapple juice. I see Uncle Randy raise his eyebrows to Aunt Ebony, as if to ask, *did I miss something?* He wipes his mouth, says, "Have you two started on your college applications? I know it's summer, but the application deadline for early decision will be here before you know it."

Imani says, "I've been working on my personal essay all week, and I've already asked two teachers for letters of recommendation."

Of course Imani is ready.

She has two schools as her top choices. I am unsure, but I would never admit that. I nod and say, "Me too. I'm almost done with my essay." I am getting really good at lying. I don't understand what the rush is. Why can't I just apply for the regular deadline? Who cares about early decision?

Imani does.

I try to eat as fast as I can so that I don't have to lie anymore. I am going over to Grandma's. I get up from the table, put my plate and silverware in the dishwasher. "Thanks for breakfast," I say.

"You're welcome," Aunt Ebony says. She looks at me with a question mark on her face, asking me with her eyes if I'm all right. I give a half-hearted smile. The doorbell rings and Imani goes to answer. Then I hear her calling my name, "Nala, Tye is here."

Tye is here?

I go to the front of the house and see Tye standing on

the stoop. When Imani sees me, she comes back into the house and I feel her look of disapproval when she walks past me.

Tye and I sit on the stoop talking and people watching. At first, it's all awkward small talk about how it's not too hot today, and then Tye gets to the reason of why he came. "I have a gift for you," he says.

"A gift?" I can't help but smile, and my heart flutters a bit. He knows how embarrassing yesterday was, so he stopped by to check on me. Tye is so thoughtful, and already I am thinking of something to get him as a thank-you.

Tye goes into his backpack and pulls out a wrapped gift. It is square and kind of heavy. I want to rip it open fast, like I usually do my Christmas presents, but I don't want to seem too anxious. I carefully open it, and when I realize what it is, I'm not sure how to respond. "Thanks— wow. A book of quotes." I hope my fake thank-you voice sounds grateful.

"I know that was a lot yesterday and you weren't pre- pared to speak, so I wanted to give you this so that the next time you have to make a speech, you can have some inspiration."

I won't ever be making a speech again. I'm not a speech- making person.

Tye is so proud of his gift he takes it from me and opens it. "Look, there are quotes from James Baldwin, Paul Robeson, Fannie Lou Hamer . . . I got this at the Schomburg Center at their gift shop."

"Thank you," I say again. Because what else can I say?

"I was thinking maybe we can go through this and find some quotes to type and blow up so we can hang them next to the photos for your photo legacy project. It would be nice to create an atmosphere in the space where you're doing the gallery."

"This is . . . this . . . thank you." That really is all I can say.

Tye is perfectly content to sit out here and look through this book of quotes all day, but I am not. I tell him I need to get to work and that I have to go. "I can walk with you," he says.

"Oh, okay, thanks." I make sure Aunt Ebony knows I am leaving, and then Tye and I walk to Grandma's. On the way he is going on about the quotes, then about how many other treasures he found at the Schomburg's gift shop and how he wants to get his mom something. I am half listening because I am trying to sort through my thoughts, trying to figure out how it is that the same characteristics that make Tye so attractive also make him frustrating. I love that he is passionate, thoughtful, that he's so respectful and just outright nice, but sometimes that passion and thought-fulness is a bit clueless and can feel condescending.

We are walking on 145th Street, and when we turn onto Edgecombe, Tye says, "You're quiet."

"Just thinking," I say.

"About what?" About us. "Nothing," I say. "Just, um, just thinking about what I'm going to do at work today." Really, I am thinking about the things Imani said to me about dating Tye. I know that the only way to prove Imani wrong is to stop pretending and start actually being the person Tye thinks I am. I don't want to be a hypocrite, and I actually do think the photo project is a good idea. Instead of lying about it, I should try to do it. And maybe I can even ask to be an official volunteer. This isn't about trying to impress Tye anymore. I really want to do it. "I'm going to start planning the photo legacy project today," I tell Tye. "Officially."

"Nice. I can't wait to see how it develops."

Yeah, me too.

When we get to Grandma's, Tye gives me a hug and I am so tempted to hold on to him, kiss him, but I know better than to do that in front of my grandma's place. I let go of him quicker than usual and say goodbye.

As soon as I get to Grandma's, I bring up the photo project again, hoping she will have some ideas on how we can really make it happen.

She's all for it. "The first thing we need to do is get that wall painted, I suppose," Grandma says. "A soft yellow would be nice, don't you think?"

"Yes, and after we paint, I can make a flyer and ask people to bring a framed photo to hang on the wall," I say. "Or maybe I can copy the photos so people can keep their originals. And if the program director has a budget, I'm sure we can find some inexpensive frames."

"Oh, right, yes. That's a better idea." Grandma smiles. "You young people just know how to put events and projects together, don't you? You, Imani . . . our future is in good hands."

I don't want her to have too much faith in me.

We leave Grandma's apartment and head to the lounge so we can tell everyone our plan. JT is the only one in the room today. He is watching an old western and drinking his sweet tea. "Miss Nala," he calls out. He gets up and walks over to me and gives me a hug, then Grandma. He holds on to her a little long and gives her a quick, soft kiss on the lips before they break away from each other. The only man I've ever seen kiss Grandma like that is Grandpa. I look away.

"Nala, tell JT about your project." Grandma has a photo album in her hand. She sets it on the table and opens it. "I know you're not ready for it yet, but I thought I'd go ahead and start looking for which photo I want on the wall."

I tell JT that I am serious about doing something with the wall, and as I tell him all about my vision for the photo legacy project, we look through Grandma's photo album. "I really like this one," JT says. He points to the one of Grandma all dressed up in her Sunday best standing outside Riverside Church. The majestic building is just as regal as Grandma, just as stoic.

"Well, thank you, JT," Grandma says. Then, real quiet, she slips in a whisper to him, "You still drinking that sugar water, huh? Doctor told you to lay off of sugar."

They start fussing, and I pretend not to hear them. I look at the wall, imagine it full of photographs, and then I head out, leaving Grandma and JT bickering. I've got to get permission to paint the wall.

I go to the main office, right at the entrance of the building. A petite brown woman is sitting at the front desk playing solitaire on her computer. When she sees me, she minimizes the screen.

I'm not sure who to ask for, so I just say, "I'd like to speak with someone about remodeling the lounge." Maybe I shouldn't have said "remodeling," because as soon as that word comes out, the woman at the desk looks at me like I have just cursed her out. "And who are you?" she asks.

We are not getting off to a good start at all.

I start over. "Sorry, my name is Nala. June Robertson is

my grandmother. She lives here. We spend a lot of time in the lounge and were wondering if we could add some warmth in it by painting one of the walls and—"

"Painting and repairs is a maintenance issue. Would you like to fill out a work order form?" She opens a drawer and pulls out a sheet of paper.

"No, I, uh—I'd like to do a photo project where residents bring a—"

"We already have our activities planned for the summer. I'm sorry."

I don't understand why I can't even get a full thought out without her interrupting me.

"If you'd like to propose an activity or a project, you need to fill out this form. We are currently taking applications for winter programs."

"Winter?"

"Yes, fall is already planned. Activities must be organized, you know. We don't do things last minute here." The woman hands me an application. I can see she has a name tag pinned onto the top of her left chest. Sharon.

"Ms. Sharon, I just want—"

Sharon clears her throat, tells me, "I've got someone waiting behind you. Anything else?"

I turn around, leave.

I walk back to the lounge slow, dreading having to tell

Grandma that we can't do the project. I don't know what's wrong with that Sharon lady. Why she couldn't just hear me out. Maybe she sees right through me, knows my secret. Maybe there's a look a true volunteer has. Maybe Imani is right—I am not made for this.

JT is in the lounge, alone. His mason jar empty of its sweet tea. "Why the sad face?" he asks. He turns the television down, which means he is expecting me to give a real answer. I can't just say *nothing* and leave the room.

I tell him about Sharon at the front desk. "I don't think we're going to be able to do the photo project," I say.

"That woman is really something else. I've been living here longer than she's been alive." JT is all riled up now. He goes on, "Folks get a little power, a little title, and think they can just treat people any ole kind of way. Even if the answer is no, she didn't have to be rude to you." JT turns the television off and opens the album Grandma left on the table. "Makes you wonder why people take the kind of jobs they do. If she doesn't like talking with people, she shouldn't work at the front desk." He flips through the album, not stopping at any of the pages until he gets to the page that only has one photo on it. It takes up the whole page. Grandma's wedding photo. JT stares at the picture. "I've heard a lot of good things about your grandpa. June tells me you two were close."

"Yeah. He was kind of like my dad since I never really had a relationship with my own."

"Your grandma sure loved him."

"Grandma talks about my grandpa to you?"

"Of course she does. Love doesn't die just because a person dies." JT turns the page. I almost grab his hand, ask him to stay there a little longer so I can see Grandpa's eyes, his smile. With the turn of the page, we are looking at baby pictures of me and Imani. Our mothers are sitting on the sofa in Grandma's old house, holding us on their laps. Even in this photo, I am trying to get away from my mother, slipping through her arms, half of me reaching for whoever is holding the camera.

"You love my grandma?" I ask. I am not usually the one to be so bold. I've been surprising myself a lot lately. Doing and saying things I'd never do.

"Why, yes. Yes, I do." JT smiles like he has just shared a secret with me. Then he starts laughing, a soft chuckle at first and then full on. "I even love her nagging." He winks.

"Sweet tea," I say.

"The only arguments we ever have," he says. "She'll have a fit if I get me some ice cream."

"You can't have ice cream?"

"Not supposed to. I can have that sugar-free junk, but that's not ice cream." JT closes the album, turns the television back on. "Those doctors have restricted every-thing I love."

"When's the last time you had ice cream?" I ask.

"Oh, months now, I think. Been so long, I can't really remember."

"And that's good. You don't need no ice cream," Grandma says.

When did she get back?

Grandma is standing in the doorway, hand on her hip. She walks across the room and sits next to JT. I wonder how long she was eavesdropping and if she heard JT say he loved her. Somehow, I think she knows even if he's never said it to her. You know when someone loves you.

"So, what's the verdict?" Grandma asks. "When do we start on our photo wall?"

"Well . . ." I tell her all about my interaction with Sha-ron. Just as I am finishing, Ms. Norma, Ms. Louise, and Ms. Mabel come in. They each take their favorite seat and join in the conversation.

Grandma is eager to fill them in. She says to me, "Tell them what happened." Her accent comes through when she is upset. She sucks her teeth and shakes her head as I tell the story for the third time. I repeat the story about the woman at the front desk who was rude and seemed unin-terested in my idea. When I finish, Ms. Norma shakes her head and says, "These new folks coming in here with no respect at all." And that sets off a whole nother conversation about all the changes that have happened since new management took over. "They act like how we did things wasn't good enough," Ms. Norma continues.

Ms. Louise nods. "There used to be a time when management asked us for our opinion on what kind of things we wanted to do around here, how we wanted the space to look. Remember that Christmas we asked them to get us a real tree instead of that small fake one they put up every year?"

"Yes, I remember," Ms. Mabel says. "That was the first time we decorated the tree together and had our own lighting ceremony right there in the lobby."

JT shakes his head. "And ever since then we get a real tree. Bet these new people don't even know that *we* started that tradition."

Ms. Norma adds, "And they don't know that we're the ones who asked for the movement classes. Wasn't it you, Louise, who got your daughter to come do a seniors' dance class for us two years ago?"

Ms. Louise seems so proud when she leans over to me and explains, "My daughter teaches at Alvin Ailey."

Ms. Norma takes a drink of water from her water bottle and says, "Had one of them young girls try to lecture me about coming to the movement class—the one we started—only now they are calling it the health and wellness class and it's yoga and meditation. Not dance."

"Bougie Black people," Ms. Mabel says.

And we all laugh, except for Ms. Mabel. She goes on, "I'm serious. And don't get me started about all these new recycling requirements."

Then Grandma says, "What you got against recycling?"

"Nobody has time for that," Ms. Mabel says.

"Now, come on, Louise," Grandma says. "We've been recycling our whole lives. You know how many butter containers I use as Tupperware?" She laughs. "And I've seen your stash of plastic bags that you reuse in your small garbage cans."

"That's recycling," JT says.

Ms. Norma is finished with her blanket. She holds it up and shows it off. We all ooh and aah and take a moment to tell her how we know her daughter is going to love this blanket. Ms. Norma looks at Ms. Mabel all serious and stern and says, "I didn't use to be so strict with recycling, but I do want to leave this world better for our children and grandchildren. I figure throwing trash in the right bin is the least I can do. We s'posed to take care of Mother Earth, s'posed to love her and leave her in good shape for the next generation."

"Well, I guess you all have a point," Ms. Mabel says. "But they need to put some respect on it. I'm their elder. I don't like that chastising tone. Mess around with me and get accidently run over by this here scooter." She rolls her eyes but then gives in to a smile.

We are laughing again—at Ms. Mabel, at bougie Black people, at the thought of Ms. Mabel running them over in her scooter. When the laughter settles and they go on to talking about something else, I think about Imani and Toya, and how a conversation with them about recycling would have quickly turned into one of them being condescending and judgmental. I think about how it definitely would not have ended in laughter. I think about how Toya called me an honorary member of Inspire Harlem, but really, sitting here with Grandma and her friends, I think maybe this is all the inspiration I need.

15

Every summer Imani and I go to at least one of the basketball tournaments at Dyckman Park. Last summer we went with Sadie and Asher. This year, Sadie can't come but Asher and Tye can. I didn't intend for this to be a double date, but here I am riding the number one train uptown to Dyckman Street. The closer we get to our stop I start seeing who's on here heading to the tournament too. I love these moments when you are riding along with strangers and then all of a sudden realize you are all going to the same place. There is something magical about a whole train of people getting off together, walking up the steps together, making a journey toward a concert, festival, or game.

We get off the train and walk the long street alongside the housing complex till we get to the park. The sun is fading just a bit so it isn't as hot as it was this afternoon, and thank goodness for that, because otherwise I'd be a sweating, hot mess. We haven't made it yet, but already I can hear music that the DJ is spinning. There's hardly space to walk, there are so many people. Boys are posted along the block checking out the girls who walk by—but pretending not to. Girls walk in groups of twos, threes, fours, some of us with intention to get to the tournament; others have that slow stride, wanting to be seen in the outfits they've been waiting to wear, even though they are trying to make it seem casual. Tye takes my hand, and it makes me feel good that he wants everyone here to know he is with me, we are together.

"Look up there," Tye says, pointing to the fire escapes on the building across the street. There are people leaning out of windows, sitting on fire escapes, perched like the crows in the morning lined up on telephone lines, watching everyone below. "They'll have a better view than we will," he says. "I don't know if we're even going to get a spot on the bleachers. We might have to stand at the gate."

The four of us squeeze our way in and are lucky enough to find good seats because people are still standing outside the court showing off, talking, dancing, so even though it's beyond crowded, not everyone has come in to get a seat. The DJ is playing all my favorite songs, and I can't keep still so I move and groove in my seat, but once Blue comes on, I can't stay seated. I get up, start dancing, and grab Tye's hand, pulling him up to dance with me.

"Come on, you know I don't dance," he says.

He tries so hard to stay seated, but I keep pulling him up. "Dance with me."

He gives in, gets up, and moves with me. We're in bleachers, so we can't go full out, but I work my hips into his, winding to the rhythm. I don't know why he doesn't dance—he definitely knows how to move, how to be easy with it, laid back, smooth.

Another song comes on, and this one brings Imani to her feet. "Yeeeess." She dances next to me, and Tye steps back to let us do our thing. Imani and I feed off each other's energy, and the row of people behind us starts dancing too. And now there are pockets of dancers showing off their moves all over the court.

The announcer comes out with a cordless microphone, hyping everyone up even more. He gets us singing along with a song the DJ is playing. Every time it gets to a certain part, the DJ mutes the music and all our voices can be heard singing at the top of our lungs. Asher and Tye stand up and join in, and we are singing and dancing together, and it is so loud, so hot, so crowded, so much like it used to be with Imani, my cousin-sister-friend.

Once the tournament starts, all eyes are on the court.

I feel like I am at a magic show, except the illusions are Black boys flying through the air, all of them wielding their very own superpower.

By the end of the game, I am hoarse from all the singing and cheering. The sun is long gone, but the mood is still celebratory. As we walk back to the train, Imani says, "This has been the highlight of summer so far."

Tye nods. "Agree."

There are so many people needing to get on the subway heading downtown that we have to let two trains pass before the four of us can fit. We get on the train, and it's too crowded to find a seat, so Tye leans against one of the doors and I lean into him. He holds on to me as we wobble along the tracks. We don't talk much as we ride until Tye says, "I don't want this night to end." In two more stops, it will be time for me to get off the train, but Tye asks me to stay on. "Don't go home yet. Stay with me."

"Stay? You mean, on the train?"

"Yeah, let's just ride."

When we get to my stop, Asher and Imani get up. "You coming?" Imani asks.

"I'll be home later. I'm . . . we're—we're just going to ride the train downtown and come back." I can tell she is surprised that I am not getting off. Usually Imani is the one staying out late, cuddled up with Asher. She smiles at me and gives me a look as if she's telling me *be-careful-have-fun-don't-stay-out-too-late* all at once. A group of people leave the train at the same time as Imani and Asher, so now there are more seats.

I sit at the window, and Tye scoots in next to me. The car is mostly empty now. I lean my head onto his shoulder. "Tell me something about you that I don't know," I say.

Tye takes my hand. He thinks for a moment, clears his throat, and says, "When my mom and dad would argue, sometimes I'd leave the house and just ride the train. I'd go all the way to the end of the line, then get up, cross over to the uptown side, and ride it back home. It was a way to clear my head. I'd do it to escape. I would just want the fighting to end. It's, uh, it feels good to do this with you for a different reason."

The train jerks to a stop. People get on, get off.

Tye says, "Your turn. Tell me something about you that I don't know."

"You don't know how insecure I really am." This might be the most honest thing I've ever said to Tye. It just comes out. Maybe because we are underground, in a tunnel, under a bustling city. Maybe because the train is half-empty and no one is paying attention to us. Maybe because I need him to know me, the real me.

Tye shifts his body and faces me. "What do you have to be insecure about? You're beauti—"

"Please don't say beautiful."

"But you are."

"I know."

Tye laughs, and I give in to a laugh too.

"I'm serious, though. People always think the only thing big girls cry about is our weight. I'm perfectly fine with my body."

"I'm sorry. I didn't mean it like that."

"I know you didn't," I tell him. "Thanks for apologizing." I kiss him on his cheek. "I don't mind you telling me I'm beautiful. Just tell me because you see it, not because you think I don't know."

"Got it," Tye says. And then, "Nala?"

"Yes?"

"You're beautiful." He kisses my cheek. "You're beautiful." He kisses my forehead. "You're beautiful." He kisses my lips.

The whole way downtown we go back and forth asking each other, "Tell me something that I don't know about you."

I tell Tye, "Okay, here's something nobody knows. Like nobody. You have to promise me you won't say anything."

"Promise."

"I don't think I want to go to college. At least, not right away. I have no idea what I want to study, what I want to be."

"That's not as bad as I thought it was going to be," Tye says. "You had me thinking you were about to confess a murder or something."

"Well, it's a big deal in my family. The Robertsons are a go-to-college kind of family. And with me being so close in age to Imani, there's even more pressure. Imani has known what she wants to be since we were little girls. A lawyer. She's always talking about how her dream is to work for the Equal Justice Initiative. She's obsessed with what Bryan Stevenson does and wants to be a part of that. And she's going to have 3.5 million things to put on her résumé for college applications because she's been volunteering since we were in middle school. Her and Asher are probably getting married one day. They're going to be that couple that's eighty and talking about how they were high school sweethearts," I say. "It's like her whole life is figured out and I don't even know what I'm doing tomorrow."

Tye sounds real serious when he says, "Okay—two things. First, tomorrow you and I are hanging out again, of course. So, um, yeah, you do know what you're doing tomorrow."

"I'm serious, Tye," I say, even with a laugh spilling out of me.

"I know, I know. Okay, for real, though, I thought

you've been working on your essay and narrowing down schools."

I forgot I told him that. "Well, yes, I am, but it's because I have to, not because I want to. And, again, I'm just saying I don't want to do the big four-year-university thing. I know I need to go to college. But I don't know what I want to study and my mom doesn't have the kind of money for college tuition, I think—"

"So wait. Is it about money? Don't you get good grades? And with all your volunteering, you should get some scholarships for sure."

"It's not only about scholarships. I don't think it's the best next step for me."

"So when are you going to tell your family?"

"I'm not. I'm going to do what's expected of me. Especially if Imani—"

"You know, you compare yourself to Imani a lot. And I get it, she's great—but so are you. Why don't you just want to be yourself?" His question punches me in my gut, knocks the wind out of me.

"I—what do you mean? What makes you ask me that?"

"I mean, it sounds like you are trying to be like Imani, to want what she wants, but what do you want? Who do you want to be?"

He isn't asking for an answer. It is the kind of question

to contemplate, to really think about and consider. I guess when you feel like you're not good enough, the next best thing is trying to be like someone else.

Tye changes the subject, and round and round we go, playing our game of questions the whole ride downtown, taking turns saying, *Tell me something about you that I don't know.*

I learn that Tye has never had surgery. I've had my tonsils and my appendix taken out.

Tye loves to cook and so do I. He's never been on a plane, but I have more times than I can count.

We both love to swim.

We both hate hiking.

The train stops, and one person gets on, then realizes this is the local train so steps off just before the doors close. We keep crawling through the tunnel, making our way downtown. By the time we get to South Ferry station, the car is empty and very few people are on the platform. We cross over to the uptown side and make our way back to Harlem. When we get on the train, Tye wraps me in his arms. I fall into a subway-sleep, where I am in a daze, half-awake, half-asleep. Every time we stop I pry my eyes open just a little and as soon as the train is in motion again, I close them. And being in Tye's arms on the one train heading to Harlem on a summer night is the only place I want to be. We are not talking about activism or community organizing, we are just being with each other, just enjoying each other.

"Nala," Tye whispers. "Our stop is next."

We get off the train and climb up the mountain of stairs back into the humid night. Neither of us wants to leave the other, so we walk the long way home.

4 THINGS I WANT TO STUDY IN COLLEGE
(IF I GO):

1. Maybe Communications
2. Maybe Photography
3. Maybe Business
4. Maybe there's a course on How To Be Yourself

16

For the first time I am at Tye's house. We are in his room, and I am surprised at how neat it is. Tye has everything in its place, and it makes me wonder if it is always like this or if he did some cleaning before I came. I am sitting in an oversized chair watching him shoot baskets in the hoop that hangs on the back of his door.

"So, what's your plan for the photo legacy project?" Tye asks.

"I don't have a plan yet. I don't even know if it's really going to happen. I have to talk with the head of programming to figure it all out." I don't have the heart to tell him it's not happening. If I tell him the photo project isn't happening, I'll have to tell him why. And telling him that I really don't work at Sugar Hill Senior Living means telling him that I've been lying to him this whole time.

"Well, it has to happen," Tye says. "It's a great idea.

And plus, isn't it your job to do programs? Why would your boss say no?"

Because it is not my job and she is not my boss.

Tye takes another shot, misses, and tries again. It goes in the second time. "I think you should make a flyer announcing what the project is and ask for residents to give you a portrait that you can copy, or you could even take a day and have people set up an appointment to get their photo taken."

"I'm not a photographer."

"But you're always taking pictures."

Tye is so into this nonexistent project.

I think maybe I should just get it over with. Tell him now that I am not—and have never been—the activity coordinator at my grandmother's residence. "Tye?"

"Yes?"

"Um, I—can we please talk about something else?" I thought I was going to tell him the truth, but I just can't say the words *Tye, I haven't been honest with you.*

Tye looks at me like he can't understand what else I could possibly want to talk about. "Can I just say one more thing?" he asks.

"One."

"I think we should start thinking about how you'll do the reveal. You could have the lounge closed for a day while we decorate and set everything up, then you can welcome all the residents in with their families and we could have some light refreshments."

"Tye—I'm not even sure if this is going to happen. And you really don't have to help me plan anything. You have your own stuff with Inspire Harlem. I don't want you to—"

"It's not a problem. I love doing these kinds of things."

Obviously.

He tosses the ball again, and I jump up off the bed and intercept it. I hold the basketball away from him.

"What are you doing?"

"I did not come over here to talk about old people and photographs." I drop the ball, lean in for a kiss. "I mean, we're dating, right?"

"Yes. Why are you asking me that?"

"Because sometimes I feel like you're more interested in helping me instead of spending time with me."

"Helping you plan the photo legacy project *is* spending time with you."

"Can we just . . . Can we just have fun? Like, what do you watch on TV?" I take the remote off the TV stand and hit the power button. I sit on his bed, tell him, "Let's just hang out." I flip through channels and see that one of my favorite reality shows is on. It follows the behind the scenes of singers as they prepare for tour. Of course, there's always drama, like the singer being sick or the backup singers not knowing their parts, even personal dramas with family, spouses, and children. I love it.

Tye says, "It's staged, though, don't you think? Is there any reality show that is actually real?"

"Just watch. It's good. And the music is the best. You get to see how artists create songs, how they plan shows." I try to sell it, but I'm not sure it's working. "Okay, just watch one episode and if you don't like it, we'll watch something else."

"All right."

Eventually there is more kissing than there is watching TV. Three episodes later, Tye is the one who is saying, "One more," and I don't gloat but inside I am smiling, and when he puts his arms around me, I lay my head on his shoulder and we spend the rest of the day in each other's arms.

By the time Tye's mom gets home, the sun is sleeping and the air is relaxed and calm. Ms. Brown has brought dinner home from their favorite restaurant and says, "Nala, it's so good to meet you. I'm glad you could come over for dinner."

"Thanks for inviting me. And nice to meet you too."

I'm not sure if I should hug her or shake her hand. Meeting people for the first time can be so awkward. We shake hands. "Can I help with anything?" I ask.

"Uh, sure. Can you set these on the dining room table?" Ms. Brown hands me two large to-go containers. When I set them on the table, I see that one is labeled Mashed Kabocha Squash, and even though I don't know what kabocha is, at least I recognize the word "squash." It's not my favorite, but I'll eat it. The other container says Teriyaki Seitan. I sound it out in my head: Sei-tan . . . say-tan . . . say-tun . . . satan? Satan as in the devil, as in opposite of light and peace, as in red suit and pitchfork? Who would eat something that literally sounds like one of the devil's nicknames? No thank you. Nope. Maybe I should have said I needed to go home for dinner.

Ms. Brown comes into the dining room carrying plates and napkins. Tye is right behind her with three glasses. "I am so hungry," she says. "Aren't you?"

Not anymore.

Tye goes back and forth from the kitchen a few times to get the pitcher of lemonade and two big serving spoons. He sits down next to me, and Ms. Brown starts dishing out the food. She gives me way too much of everything, and as she piles the food on my plate, she explains, "I love kabocha squash. It's so much sweeter than butternut."

I'm a little relieved knowing I'll at least like the mashed squash. But still, what is seitan?

We all start eating. I take a bit of the teriyaki seitan, and it's only because I have good home training that I don't spit it out back onto the plate. What is this? Ms. Brown must notice the look on my face. "Not a fan of seitan?" she asks. "Maybe I should have ordered tofu."

"Oh, no. It's totally fine. This is . . . this tastes . . . this is good. Perfect." I take a big bite and hardly chew, just swallow it as fast as I can so I don't have to taste it. At least the teriyaki sauce gives it some flavor. I feel like I am seven years old and at Grandma's kitchen table sneaking food into my napkin that I don't want to eat.

As we eat, Ms. Brown tells me all kinds of stories about Tye, and I love learning about him through someone else's eyes. Somehow I manage to eat most of my food. There's an appropriate amount left on my plate, an amount that says *I'm too full to eat another bite* instead of *This was the worst meal I've ever had*.

"So, tell me, Nala, how's your summer going?" Ms. Brown asks.

Can I tell her that because of her son it is the best summer I've ever had? "It's good," I say.

"Tye told me you work as a volunteer at Sugar Hill Senior Living."

This isn't a question, but I answer with, "Yes, I am. I'm over the Open Studio."

Ms. Brown tilts her head just a bit, in a way that says a big question is coming. "That's so interesting, I didn't know they had an activity coordinator. My friend's mother lives there. The way she talks, new management came and they don't have any good activities anymore. She's so funny, always talking about running people over with her scooter. I wonder why she doesn't go to any of your activities."

I take another bite of this nasty, satanic food just so I don't have to answer right away.

Tye answers instead. "It's new, Mom. Nala just started this summer."

"Oh, I see," Ms. Brown says. She is talking to Tye, but her eyes are on me. "Will you still work there during the school year, or is this just a summer job?"

I take a sip of lemonade. "I, uh, I haven't decided." I do not look Ms. Brown in the eyes.

"Well, I'd love to have you meet my friend's mom. I'll try to remember to tell her to look for you. Just in case some random person comes up to you, her name is Ms. Mabel. You won't forget her once you meet her," Ms. Brown says.

I look up at the mention of Grandma's friend. I do not say that I know her, but my eyes must be saying something to Ms. Brown because she leans forward and asks, "Does that name sound familiar?"

"I—I think so—yes. I think my grandmother might know her." I take my phone out of my pocket and pretend to check the time. "I'm so sorry. I didn't realize how late it is. I need to get going soon. Thanks so much for dinner, Ms. Brown. It was really good."

"You're welcome. Come back anytime," she says. She pushes her chair away from the table and gets up to hug me. "Tye, are you walking her home?"

"Yes," he says.

Ms. Brown is just like Aunt Ebony and Grandma and all the women in my family—there are certain questions that are not questions at all. You can always tell by the tone, by the look in her eyes that really, it is a command not a request.

Tye takes the dishes into the kitchen, and while we wait for him, Ms. Brown walks me to the door, gives me a hug, and says, "My son really likes you. He talks so highly of you. I'm glad he has someone like you."

17

I sleep in today and don't get out of bed till eleven o'clock. Okay, that's not super late but in this house, we rise and shine early. By the time I shower and get dressed, Imani is already gone. Aunt Ebony is dressed and looks like she's been gone and back again because her keys are on the counter instead of the usual hook they hang on at the door.

I scramble eggs and make toast, and just when I am about to walk out the door to meet Tye, Aunt Ebony asks, "Where are you heading?"

"Out with Tye," I say.

"Have you worked on your college essay?" she asks. "Don't let the summer go by with nothing to show for it, Nala. You have such good grades, and you did very well on your SAT. You have some great choices for school. Do you need me to help with anything?"

"I'm fine," I say.

Aunt Ebony knows me so well. She says, "You haven't started, have you?"

I can't lie to her. I can't. "I'm going to be finished by the end of summer. I promise."

"Are you stuck?"

"I wouldn't say that," I tell her. "I'm just, I'm brainstorming right now. My English teacher said making random lists is a way to get ideas about what you want to write about. So right now, I'm just in the beginning phase, just thinking and making lists about my life until something, I don't know . . . until something—"

"Resonates?"

"Right."

Aunt Ebony gives me a look like she isn't quite sure she trusts my answer.

"I'm serious," I tell her. "Our teacher told us that colleges like personal essays about lessons learned or important, life-changing moments. So I'm just thinking of what I might want to write about. I've been making lists in my notebook."

She just looks at me. "Don't lose yourself in that boy," she says.

Yeah, she knows me. Maybe better than I know myself.

Tye sends me a text that he's a block away, so I go outside to meet him. We don't have a plan, so we just start walking. We stop at the bodega. He gets a bag of chips—plain (not even with ridges), and I get a bottled water and a candy bar for later.

We wander to 135th and Fifth, and I see a Goodwill store. "Can we stop in here?" I ask.

"Goodwill?"

"Yes, they have good deals on cute clothes sometimes." I pull his arm and walk him into the store. We browse the aisles, not really looking for anything in particular. I look through the clothes and stick to my try-it-if-you-like-it rule because sometimes tags are deceiving and I can actually fit a size that in other stores I can't. I grab a few cute summer skirts and try them on. Two out of four fit. Not bad. I look for tops and only find one that I really like—and that really fits. When I come out of the dressing room, I don't see Tye and then I realize that he is trying on clothes too.

"Be out in a minute," he calls out.

"See, I told you there are good deals here."

Tye laughs and opens his door. "What do you think of this?" He pretends to be a model—he doesn't have to try hard. He is wearing a navy shirt, and even though it is simple, I tell him he should definitely get it. It looks good on him. Everything looks good on him.

We take a shortcut down the housewares section to get to the cashier. At the end of the aisle, I see a row of frames of different sizes. They all look antique, golden treasures waiting to hold a memory. "These would be perfect for the photo legacy project," Tye says.

I keep walking because it is not happening and I do not need to buy any frames.

"Did you hear me, Nala? Hold up."

I stop, turn around.

Tye has one of the frames in his hand. "Look at this. Only two dollars. We should get some."

I walk over to him, look through the shelf, picking a few up that look so precious, so one-of-a-kind. There are five that I love, and Tye says, "You have to get them."

I stand there. *Tell him, Nala. Tell him.*

I can't. I just can't. He is too excited and he is too into me and I am too into him and I can't tell the person who hates liars that I've been lying and I can't tell the person whose father always cancels plans that there is no plan. I can't ruin it all, ruin us.

So we shop for frames, and we leave the Goodwill in Harlem and go to another Goodwill because Tye says, "The one on the Upper West Side might have vintage frames too. Let's just get as many as we can today."

And when we leave that Goodwill, we go to one more, and then Tye takes me to a party supply store that he swears has the best prices and we buy decorations for a room we will not adorn and we buy plates and cups for the refreshments no one will eat or drink.

Maybe I can get Sharon to change her mind. Maybe.

We head back uptown. It is too hot to take the train, so we get on the bus. The whole ride to Harlem, I am thinking, *What if Sharon doesn't change her mind? What will I do with all these frames and decorations and plates?*

We get off the bus, head home. The totes are heavy, and I can't figure out if it's more comfortable to carry mine on my shoulder or in my hands. I keep switching back and forth, and then Tye takes the bag out of my hand and says, "I got it." He carries all the bags, except the one with my clothes. He even brings them upstairs to my room once we are at my house. "Let me know when you want to do round two. We're going to need more frames."

We.

"Okay, I'll let you know," I tell him. I whisper a prayer that somehow Sharon has a change of heart.

Before Tye leaves, he stops and says, "Don't make any plans for this Thursday evening."

"Why? What's up?"

"I'm taking you on a date. No Inspire Harlem talk, no Sugar Hill Open Studio talk."

"What are we going to do?"

Tye kisses me on my cheek. "It's a surprise."

18

For the next two days, I follow Aunt Ebony's advice and try to work on my essay. Even though I don't know where I want to go or what I want to study, I know eventually I'm going to have to do this, so I might as well get started. I try to come up with a topic for my personal essay, but nothing comes to mind. Nothing. I feel like I wasted two days just staring at my notebook of lists, staring at my laptop, typing over and over: *I don't know what to write. I don't know what to write.*

Since I couldn't write anything, I spent time looking over my notes. Our guidance counselor said CUNY schools are a great option and that I should look into one of them. So that's how I spend the last hours of my two-day break from Tye. Making lists of schools I might want to go to, right here in New York. Thinking about college makes me wonder what Tye's plan is. We've never talked about where he wants to go, what he wants to be. I'm kind of afraid to ask him. Maybe it's better to hold on to this summer, to let these days exist without any talk of leaving each other, of not being together.

Thursday is here, and it's brought butterflies with it. No matter how much time I spend with Tye, I am still nervous and excited when I know I am about to see him. He sent a text asking me to meet him on 135th at the C subway station. As we go underground I ask, "Where are you taking me? Can I at least get a hint?"

"We're going to Brooklyn."

"Brooklyn?"

Tye steps aside so I can go through the turnstile. "You have something against Brooklyn?"

"The C all the way to Brooklyn?" I ask.

"The longer we get to spend time together." Tye can be a little corny sometimes, but I love it. We get to the platform and wait for the train. Tye pulls me in to him, then runs his fingers through my braids.

The train pulls into the station. We get on, find seats, and bump and jerk our way downtown. There is the usual subway commotion going on: a person asking for change, someone singing for change, three break-dancers spinning for change. People move about trying to find a seat, trying to make it out of the sliding door before it closes, a toddler mimicking the *ding* of the closing doors every single time, the man nodding off then jumping up in terror thinking he missed his stop.

Tye doesn't seem to notice any of it. His eyes are on me, and he is talking with me as if no one else is around. "I, uh, I got you something. It's not like a big deal or anything, it's just a little something I picked up the other day." Tye sounds nervous, and now my heart is fluttering and my hands are sweating. "Here." He goes into his backpack and takes out a slender rectangular box. So right away I know it's not jewelry—I mean, not that I thought it was or anything. I'm just saying I definitely know it's not. The box isn't wrapped in wrapping paper, but it's not obvious what it is.

"Can I open it now?" I ask.

"Oh yeah. It's not a big deal at all."

Tye doesn't know that I have never received a gift from a guy except my grandpa and Uncle Randy. Oh, and a valentine from a boy named Coby in the fourth grade. And in one month, I am now getting my second gift from my boyfriend. Um, this is kind of a big deal. I open the box, and the first thing I see is a shiny silver circle. I pull it up out of the box and realize that shiny silver circle is the top to a sleek, black water bottle.

"It's double walled, stainless steel. You can use it for hot or cold beverages."

I want to say something, but no words are coming.

Tye continues, "It's been rated as the best water bottle for the past three years. It has a leak-free top and it doesn't sweat and it'll keep the temperature of the beverage—or any liquid, actually, like soup or something—for at least twenty-four hours."

Tye stops talking, waiting for me to say something.

Then, he adds, "I notice that you're always buying bottled water at the bodega, so I thought I'd get you one of these."

I can't even fake a thank-you. I just, I can't. First a book of quotes and now a water bottle.

"Are you, are you okay? Is the color wrong—I know it's black, but I figured black would—"

"I don't care that it's black, Tye." I say this sharp and with so much attitude the woman across from us looks at us in shock, like I startled her. I lower my voice. "I—well, first of all, thank you. But—"

"But? Who says *but* when saying thank you to a gift from their boyfriend?" Now Tye is raising his voice a little, and we are officially having our first argument. Over. A. Water. Bottle. *Let it go, Nala*, I tell myself. And I do. I let it go until Tye says, "You don't look happy."

"Why would I be happy about my boyfriend chastising me about not drinking out of a reusable water bottle? I mean, I don't know—we're on a date. Who knew double walled, stainless steel was so romantic?"

Tye scoots away from me. Not a lot, but enough for me to notice that he moved, that the energy between us shifted. "I thought you'd appreciate that I was thinking of you." Tye sounds so sincere when he says this that all the irritation in me dissolves and I feel so selfish for being ungrateful.

I look the water bottle over, read the little square tag that's wrapped around the top. "Thank you," I say. "And you're right. I don't have one of these."

Tye still looks like a sad puppy, so I add, "And I like the color black, so yeah, thanks."

We ride the rest of the way in an awkward silence. I wonder what Tye is thinking about. I am daydreaming of things I wish Tye had given me.

GIFT IDEAS FOR YOUR NEW GIRLFRIEND

1. Flowers. I know, I know. Total cliché, right? But I actually really do like flowers. And I don't need a dozen roses, just a simple bouquet of something to brighten up my day. Something that says, *these are lovely and so are you.*

2. A handwritten note. The more personal the better, but as I've discovered, the right quote can go a long way, so even if it's a poem or song lyrics that aren't original—as long as they're heartfelt, I'm okay with that.

3. A framed photo of the two of us. Tye and I have 1.7 million selfies of our summer outings. It would be nice to see at least one of them off a screen.

4. Time. Giving time is the most valuable gift. I don't really need Tye to give me something tangible. Spending the summer together is the gift I didn't know I wanted, needed.

High Street is announced over the intercom as the next stop. "This is us," Tye says. He stands and wobbles to the door. I wait for the train to stop. The humidity greets us as soon as we get off the subway. It is sticky and hot underground, and there are too many smells clashing with one another to make out what any of them are. But the closer I walk to Tye, the more I smell his cologne. We climb the stairs, me a little out of breath, but I don't ask him to stop. I keep up, follow his lead.

"I never come to this part of Brooklyn," I admit. "It's

quieter over here, feels less crowded and busy." I say this hoping it is a peace offering, hoping we're not still in our funk.

"I'm taking you to Brooklyn Bridge Park. The whole month of July they're showing movies here every Thursday evening," Tye tells me. "There's only two more screenings, and I thought you'd like tonight's flick. Thought it would be cool to watch a movie with a view. Got a blanket and some snacks in my bag. Hope this is an okay plan."

"This is perfect," I say.

We walk through DUMBO, making our way to the park. The annoyance and irritation between us is gone. Tye takes my hand, and when we turn the corner I can barely focus on anything else but the majestic view of the Manhattan Bridge. I can tell that we're getting closer to the park because there are more people. We have to walk single file, me behind Tye, to get down the block. Once we enter the park, we are side by side again holding hands, and then I see the Brooklyn Bridge and downtown Manhattan looking close enough to touch. The East River splashes against the oversized stones, and now that we're at the water, it feels a little cooler. We walk around, and after taking it all in we claim a spot and put the blanket down. "How'd I do?" Tye asks.

"I'm loving everything about tonight," I tell him.

The sun is yawning its way into night. The movie will start once it's dark, so we eat and watch the city lights shimmer on the river water. As dusk settles, more and more families, couples, and groups find a spot on the lawn. Now that we aren't arguing anymore, I take my phone out and take photos of the Brooklyn Bridge, then a few shots of the crowd that is forming on the grass and steps of the park. We take a few selfies, and then Tye grabs my phone and starts taking candids of me. "Tye!" I reach for it, but he is not giving it up. "Why can't I take pictures of you?" He takes a few more. Then shows them to me. "See, you're beautiful," he says.

"Thank you," I say. "And so are you."

"Beautiful? Don't you mean handsome?"

"Nope. You. Are. Beautiful," I tell him. "Beauty is not just a word for girls, you know." I rub my hand against his face, trace his eyebrows, ease my hand to his head and draw random shapes with the tips of my fingers all the way to the nape of his neck.

Tye lies back, his face looking at the changing sky. We lounge together, taking in the view, taking in each other. Then, Tye sits up, says, "I forgot to ask—how are things going with the photo legacy project? When are we going to get the rest of the frames?"

I tell him half of the truth. "Sharon, my, um,

boss—she won't let it happen. I'm not going to be able to do it." When I say this, part of me is relieved. And then, I realize that I can just end the whole lie right now without ever letting Tye know it was a lie. "I think I'm just going to step down, end the Open Studio, and stop working there," I tell Tye. "Maybe I'll join Inspire Harlem."

I have been thinking about getting involved in something for real. I can do without Toya, but as long as Tye, Imani, and Sadie are there, I think I could manage.

He sits up. "You can't quit. You can't just give up."

I hear applause and realize the movie is starting. "We can talk about this later," I whisper.

"You can't quit, Nala. Don't take no for an answer. If it's something the residents want, something you feel passionate about, you have to fight for it." Tye is always so confident, so sure.

"Can we please just talk about this later?" I ask. The couple next to us hushes us, and the woman in front of me turns around and rolls her eyes. A little girl whines to her father about not being able to hear, and we are hushed again.

Tye lowers his voice but keeps talking, "Nala, seriously. We can't call ourselves activists or community organizers if we don't do the work."

I don't call myself an activist or community organizer.

"Tye, please! Can we let it go for now? We're on a date, aren't we? Why can't we just enjoy the movie? Somehow you manage to make everything a social justice moment—"

"What is your problem? All I'm trying to do is encourage you to do the thing you say you love so much." Tye is loud-whispering, which is just as annoying as if he were yelling.

"Can we *please* just watch the movie? That's all I'm asking."

"Why are you so grumpy all of a sudden?"

"I'm not grumpy. I just want to have fun with my boyfriend. I don't want to talk about volunteering at my grandmother's residence. And I definitely don't want to discuss what *Consumer Reports* has to say about the best water bottle on the market."

Tye rubs his head, exhales a deep breath, and looks at the screen. We watch the movie, but we don't watch it together, not like a couple watches a movie. There is no hand holding, no joining in on the laughter, no grabbing each other if something scary happens.

Just when I am relaxing and getting into the movie, letting the argument go, Tye leans over to me and says, "If you don't want the water bottle, just give it back."

"It's not about if I want the water bottle, Tye!"

"Well, what is it about?"

I get up, take the water bottle out of my bag, and throw it on the blanket. "It's about me not wanting to feel like you want to change me, or make me into someone I'm not. These gifts aren't about me, they're about you—it irritates you that I buy bottled water, so you—"

"Excuse me, uh, we're trying to watch the movie," a woman whispers.

I feel so much shame for making a scene. I walk away, tiptoeing across the tiny patches of grass not covered by sheets and blankets. I am not crying but I want to. I walk outside the park, cross the street. Once I am across the street, I turn around thinking Tye is behind me, thinking now we can talk without bothering people. But when I turn around, Tye is not there.

19

8 TEXT MESSAGES I ALMOST SEND TO TYE

1. I wasn't really upset. April Fools . . . even though it's not April. #JulyIsTheNewApril #JustKidding #AndTheOscarGoesTo

2. Tye, please call me. Please let's talk.

3. I'm not sure how this became my fault. I asked if we could talk about it later, and you kept pushing it. At the park you had so much to say, but now you're giving me the silent treatment?! Really?!

4. Are we just arguing, or does this mean we've broken up?

5. I didn't mean to hurt your feelings.

6. Tye, I'm not who you think I am, and I can't keep pretending.

7. Here's something you don't know about me: I've been lying to you.

8. I'm sorry.

Tye didn't text or call me last night, not even to see if I made it home. I haven't heard from him today either. I try to distract myself, keep my mind off him. Uncle Randy always says, when you're feeling bad about your circumstances you should do something kind for someone. So, I decide to get out of the house, do something kind for JT.

I am at Grandma's, standing at the front desk with an ice cream sundae in my hand. "Can you tell me what apartment JT Dixon is in?" I ask. I realized on my way over here that I've never been to JT's apartment. He's always sitting out in the lounge. I have no idea where he lives.

"Isn't June Robertson your grandmother?" Ms. Sharon asks.

"Yes, I am here to see her too, but first I need to drop this off at JT's." I am sneaking this treat to him. If Grandma finds out that I'm giving him ice cream, I don't think she'll ever forgive me.

Ms. Sharon doesn't even look at me when she says, "I'm not allowed to share personal information about residents."

And I get it. It's probably not safe to just let random strangers know where residents live, but I am not random. She knows who I am, and if I was going to hurt JT, would I be announcing myself and bringing him dessert?

"Why don't you ask your grandmother where he lives?" Sharon says, and then the phone rings, so she picks it up and that's that, until I see Ms. Louise, who waves me down the hallway and motions for me to come to her.

I do not want Grandma to see me holding this ice cream. I look around, make sure she is nowhere in sight. I walk over to Ms. Louise, and as soon as she sees the ice cream in my hand, she says, "Oh, you come bearing gifts today?"

I laugh. "I only have one this time," I say.

"Well, I guess that's okay," she says. "You looking for your grandma? If she's not in the lounge or her apartment, check JT's place. Fifth floor, apartment 5A."

Perfect. I didn't even have to ask. "Thank you." I get on the elevator in a hurry, hoping the ice cream doesn't melt any more than it already has.

I knock on JT's door and wait and wait. I really hope he's home and not at Grandma's. I put my ear to the door, and I can hear the television—on one of the westerns, of course. I knock again, harder this time. JT opens the door, and I'm not even sure if he sees me. His eyes are fixed on the ice cream. "For me? You bought this for me?"

I hand the sundae to him. "Everyone deserves a sweet cold treat, especially in the summertime."

"Miss Nala, you are too kind. Too kind, indeed." With JT's door cracked open I get a glimpse of his apartment. It is a similar layout as Grandma's, but he has a lot less furniture, fewer photos on the wall. Makes me wonder what picture he would've shared for the project that isn't happening anymore. JT smiles. "Your grandmother know about this?"

"Nope."

He opens the door all the way. "Come in," he says. JT becomes a little child, the way he rushes to get a spoon, the way he takes the cherry off the top and devours it. "How'd you know hot fudge is my favorite?"

I shrug. "Who doesn't like hot fudge?"

"Indeed, Miss Nala. Indeed." We sit at the kitchen table. JT digs into his sundae. "Now, isn't this a shame—I don't have anything special to offer you. Would you like some sweet tea?"

"No thank you," I say.

JT eats a few spoonfuls and then asks, "So, what's on your mind today?"

"Nothing."

"That's impossible," JT says.

I laugh. I guess he's right. It's kind of impossible to think about absolutely nothing. I ask JT, "Do you think I should still try to do the photo project?"

"Oh, so that's what's on your mind."

"Yeah, I'm thinking maybe I gave in too easy. Maybe I should have tried harder." I've been thinking a lot about what Tye said. I still think we could have waited to talk about it. But he has a point. That's what's on my mind. I am thinking about how I spent the first two weeks of summer lounging on the sofa and streaming movies all day. And now, here I am actually wanting to volunteer and do something important with my time.

"It's not too late," JT says. "Persistence can get you far."

And just like that I've decided to find a way to do this.

There's a knock at the door, and JT calls out, "Who's there?"

"It's me," Grandma says.

JT scrapes the last bit of ice cream out of the plastic cup and throws it away. He puts his index finger up to his mouth. "Shh. Our secret."

I whisper, "Our secret."

He opens the door.

"Well, what are you doing here?" Grandma asks.

"I, um—"

"She came to see you, but I pulled her in here because I wanted to talk to her about the photo project. We've been talking about her giving it another go," JT says.

"Well, I am glad to hear that. I think that's a great idea."

As Grandma gets settled, I stand and push in my chair. "I'm going to go see if I can set up a meeting with Ms. Sharon. I'll be right back."

I leave JT's apartment and head to the main office. This time, I have a plan. I just want to ask for a meeting. I think setting up a formal time to talk where I can really share my idea is better than just blurting it out at the front desk when there's a line forming. I'm almost at the front desk when I feel my phone buzzing in my pocket. Tye is calling. I wanted to call him first, be the one to apologize and ask if we could talk. I answer the phone. "Hello?"

"Hey, where are you?"

"At work," I say.

And then I hear Imani's voice. "You mean, at Grandma's?"

"What?" I ask. And then I turn the corner and see Tye and Imani standing at the front desk. Ms. Sharon is there too, and they are all looking at me with contempt in their eyes. I hang up the phone. "I can explain," I say.

Tye turns around and walks out the door.

"You lied about working here?" Imani says. She says more, but I run after Tye so I don't hear her full rebuke.

"Tye, please. Let me explain."

Tye stops and turns around slow. "Do you work here or not?"

"No."

Tye starts to walk away again.

"Wait. Just—just let me explain."

Tye stops walking, but he doesn't face me. People bump into him because he is standing still in the middle of the sidewalk. He doesn't move. "You give me updates all the time about how things are going at work; we've been shopping for the photo project . . . I don't understand why you're playing games with me. All this talk about you wanting to get to know each other, and the whole time you've been lying to me? Has everything between us been a lie?"

"Everything? No. Not my feelings for you. No."

"How can I believe you?" Tye walks away.

"Tye!"

He keeps walking.

"Tye!"

He turns the corner, gone.

I didn't cry yesterday when we argued, and I didn't cry when I turned around and saw he wasn't coming back to

Harlem with me. I didn't cry on the subway on the long ride uptown, or in bed that night when I replayed every moment we've ever spent over and over. I haven't cried at all until right now. No words will come out of me, just tears. And I can't stop them.

20

WORST PLACES TO CRY

1. At the park in front of all the kids who just watched the neighborhood bully push you off the swing.

2. In the nurse's office when you are in the sixth grade and realize your period has started and everyone, including the cute guy you have a crush on, knows.

3. On a New York City subway when you thought you were grown enough to take the train by yourself but missed your stop and panicked because you realized your mom was right, you weren't ready. And she knew this, so she was on

the train, just a few seats away waiting for you to
need her.

4. On a sidewalk, standing alone, watching your
boyfriend walk away.

When I step back into the lobby, Ms. Sharon is waiting
there with her arms folded looking like she is about to
scold me. And Imani must've called for Grandma because
she's here too and so are all her friends and JT. "What is
this Imani is telling me about you pretending to work
here?" Grandma asks.

I roll my eyes at Imani.

"Grandma, she did all of this to get a guy to like
her—"

"I can talk for myself, Imani. And what did you do, go
and tell Tye I wasn't woke enough so you could hook him
up with Toya?"

"What? No. Tye came by the house looking for you,
and when I told him you weren't home, he asked me if you
were at work. I thought he was confused or something
because you definitely don't have a job, but it turns out not
only is she jobless, she's also a liar and a fraud."

Ms. Norma and Ms. Mabel are looking at me with
disappointed eyes. JT too.

Grandma stands between us. "All right, enough. We're making a scene," Grandma says. "Let's talk about this in private." She walks away, and Imani and I follow her.

Ms. Mabel looks at me, and I know that this means she's already known the truth. I wonder why she hasn't said anything. Not even to me. She isn't frowning or looking disappointed, she's actually looking kind and warm, like she wants to reach out and give me a hug, but I keep walking, following Grandma and Imani down the hall.

As soon as we get into Grandma's, Imani starts up again. "I don't understand you, Nala. Do you just need attention or something? What's been going on with you lately?"

I don't feel like I owe Imani an explanation at all. But Grandma sits down in her rocking chair and says, "Well, answer her."

"No, I didn't do it to get attention. I actually, I—at first I was just, yeah, I was trying to impress Tye. I like him and he's so involved in the community, I wanted him to like me."

"So you pretended to care about me? My friends?" Grandma's voice has never sounded this disappointed, not at me anyway.

"No—I care about you, Grandma. I love spending time here. And yes, at first I exaggerated the truth about me being here, but the photo project . . . I—I really do want to do that. I do."

Grandma just sighs a deep sigh. Then Imani says, "I don't believe you."

"Well, that's the truth."

"No, Nala. The truth is, you're jealous of me. It's not enough that you moved into *my* house, claiming *my* mother as your own. You have to have *my* friends too."

And the way she says *my* makes me wonder if there will ever be a *we* again—no more Imani and Nala, cousin-sister-friends.

"Imani, watch yourself," Grandma says.

But Imani keeps talking. "Grandma, she's been rude to my friend Toya, and she's got Sadie braiding her hair, and she's tricked Tye into—"

"The fact that you are saying this just shows how selfish you really are, Imani." I am yelling, and so I lower my voice, calm myself. "I get it now. You're mad because your friends actually like me. You didn't think I was good enough to fit with your friends, but I am. And you don't know what to do with that. I mean, who are you if you're not the cousin who does everything better than Nala?" I say. "Well, sorry to burst your I'm-Woke-I'm-an-Ally-I'm-Socially-Conscious-I'm-Better-Than-You bubble . . . people actually like me. You're not the only one in this family who can have friends or have attention from a hot guy."

"Everything is always about you, Nala. For once, just

once, I want to have a life outside of the two of us. My own friends, time to do what I want to do. I have always had to look out for you. Always consider Nala's feelings." Imani's voice is trembling like she is on the verge of tears, like a glass teetering on the edge. She breaks, crashes down into shattered tears. "You keep wondering why I don't spend time at home . . . it's because my own mother gives you more attention than she does me."

I stand up, put my shoes back on. "I never, never tried to take Aunt Ebony away from you. If you didn't want me living with you—"

"All right, enough! Enough, I said." Grandma never yells at us. Never. "Nala, where do you think you're going?"

"Anywhere but here," I say. And Grandma gives me a look like I better sit myself down and fix my attitude. I don't test her. I take my shoes back off. Sit down. But instead of sitting on the sofa, anywhere near them, I sit at the dining room table. I can still see them, hear them.

"I don't know what's gotten into the two of you, but you both have got to figure it out. We don't do this."

We. I am still a part of Grandma's *we*. She's mad at me, but not so much that she's stopped loving me, wanting me.

"You both thinking you know everything, thinking you're right. Well, you're both wrong." Grandma turns to Imani and says, "Life can't be about trying to prove a point, or making someone feel less than you. You walking around having love for the planet, love for animals, love for every outcast, downtrodden person, but you ain't got no love for your cousin? For your momma? Me? Since when you so high and mighty that you don't come to family gatherings? Since when? You think you're smart and brave and passionate? Who you think taught you to be that way?"

Tell her, Grandma, tell her.

"And Nala Robertson, you have got to start learning how to love yourself. For you, it will always be easier to love other people, to put them first and cater to them, to adapt to their needs. You want to really be something in this world—learn how to walk in a room being yourself and staying true to who you are. Yes, there's room for growth, always. But if the change isn't for you it won't last."

Imani has her head down, her arms folded.

Grandma gets up, goes into the kitchen, and brings out two bottles of Ting and sets them on the dining room table. Then, she goes back into the kitchen and shakes out plantain chips into a bowl. She sets the bowl in the middle of the table. Grandma walks to the door, slips her sandals on, and before she leaves, she says, "You two are family. Family. That alone ought to be enough for you to respect each other. You're also two women. Black women. The most radical thing you can do is love yourself and each other."

We sit and sit. Me sipping the grapefruit soda Grandma left out for us every few minutes and nibbling on the chips. Imani stays in the living room on the sofa. Thirty minutes have passed, and we haven't said anything to each other. But I can see that Imani's shoulders have relaxed, that her eyes aren't burning a curse through me anymore. Her phone is buzzing; so is mine. But we don't answer them. Somehow, I think we both know that Grandma would not approve of us answering a phone call or responding to a text. Not now.

We sit and sit.

I finish my soda.

Forty-five minutes.

Grandma is still gone, and we still haven't said a word to each other. I see Imani's eyes looking at Grandma's open Bible. She is reading it, I can tell. I wonder what it says today. Every now and then, our eyes meet and linger on each other, and when I look at her, I see past what she said today, past how cold she's been all month. I see way back to when we were kids and summers were spent splashing in fire hydrants and spending all our allowance at the Coco Helado carts. I see her greeting me at the door when I showed up at her doorstep soaking wet with rain and snot and tears, how she hugged me even though I was wet and falling apart. How she was the one to say, *Mom, can she live here?*

I see all of that. She is still that person too.

I'll hold on to that, hope she has some good memories about me to hold on to.

21

I am lying in my bed waiting.

The sun is awake and bright and enveloping my room. It is time to get up, but I stay in bed because I hear Imani moving around and I don't want to see her. Not yet. Last night we never did speak, not even when Aunt Ebony picked us up from Grandma's, not even when she asked us what was going on. We were silent the whole way home, and I went straight to my room (with nothing to eat, by the way) and went to bed.

This morning, I am listening to Blue and she is getting me in a better mood. I sing along, distract myself from the fact that I really need to use the bathroom. And I mean in that first-thing-in-the-morning kind of way that is really hard to hold. But I wait. I twist my legs shut, hold it. I can hear everything Imani is doing. First, her five-minute shower and now she must be drying off. I hear the mirror to the medicine cabinet open, then close. She must be getting her hair products out. There is a pause, and the medicine cabinet opens and closes again. Then, finally, the bathroom door opens and she walks out. I hear her bedroom door open, close.

I wait.

The door opens and closes again. Imani runs back to the bathroom, grabs something, and rushes back to her bedroom.

I don't move.

There's music playing from her room, and I figure she must be getting dressed. Soon enough I'll be able to get up, go to the bathroom. If not, I'll have to get over it because I am too old to wet the bed. I stand up, pace the room (does that really help?), and try to distract myself while I wait for her to leave. I do not want any accidental hallway run-ins. I pull the cord to the charger out of my phone and check my notifications. No text from Tye, no missed calls. I toss the phone back on the bed.

The doorbell rings, and I hear Imani running down the stairs. Then, Asher's voice is booming through the house with Aunt Ebony's. They all talk for a while. I can't make out what they are saying, but their voices are loud and constant. Then, the front door opens, closes.

Imani is gone.

I run to the bathroom, don't even close the door.

Relief.

I shower and get dressed and listen to see if Aunt Ebony is still here. I hear her walking back and forth from the kitchen to the living room, so I decide to stay upstairs a little longer. I am not ready to talk with her either.

I sit on my bed, pick my phone up, and scroll through Instagram. Sadie has posted a photo of me, her, and Imani at her house from the day she braided my hair. I tap the heart to like it and keep scrolling. I am looking to see if Tye has posted anything.

Nothing.

I go to his page; maybe I missed it. I look over his posts and see he hasn't been on since the last picture he shared— the one of me and him at Brooklyn Bridge Park. I don't like it or make a comment. I just stare at it. Tap it and zoom in on his face. His eyes are smiling in this picture. I wonder if I'll ever look into his eyes again, ever be in his arms like that.

I go to Inspire Harlem's page, and there are no new photos here either, just the recap of the community block party. I swipe through them: a photo of Asher and Tye setting up, one of the massive crowd, and there's even a photo of all the tote bags on the table, stuffed and ready to go.

Seeing this photo makes me realize I never looked

inside my tote. It's been on the floor of my closet since I came home that day. I go to my closet, get the bag, and dump everything out. There are coupons to local stores, bookmarks, stickers, hand sanitizer, and tons of brochures. There's also a postcard-sized flyer that has Inspire Harlem's core tenets listed with a mural behind the words.

Remember Harlem.

Honor Harlem.

Critique Harlem.

Love Harlem.

I pin it to the corkboard that hangs beside my desk. I stand in front of my mirror, put my braids up in a ponytail, and pick my phone back up. I scroll and scroll. Still no posts from Tye. I think about leaving a comment under the picture, but what can I say?

I waste about thirty minutes looking through Tye's photos. Besides the picture of us, one of my favorites is the one of him with his mom. Someone caught them in a candid moment—a hug that looks so genuine, so tight. The caption says, Me and my first love. I get caught up on Tye's page and then snap out of it, deciding that I can't stay in my room all day obsessing over him. I get out of Instagram, call Grandma, and make a plan to come over.

By the time I am downstairs, Aunt Ebony is already gone. I feel relief, even though I think maybe she will understand why I lied about everything. I grab an apple and leave. The whole way to Grandma's I rehearse the apology I know I need to give her.

There is no apologizing when I get to Grandma's because when I step into the lobby, she is fussing at Ms. Sharon and all her friends are there, adding on. This is not Grandma's I'm-fussing-because-I-love-you rant, this is something else. "How dare you move my puzzle without my permission. And you didn't even keep it intact?"

"Got some nerve," Ms. Mabel shouts.

Ms. Sharon is talking in a calm but stern voice. "The rules of the lounge state that every person needs to clean up after themselves. No one is allowed to take up space for an extended amount of time."

Ms. Norma scolds Ms. Sharon. "Ain't nothing wrong with June doing her puzzle in the lounge. Any resident can contribute to it, so what's the big deal?"

"The big deal is that the rules are—"

Grandma puts her hand on her hip and talks in the same calm but stern voice as Ms. Sharon. "I know what the rules say, but the norms are that in this building we respect each other's property. The norms are that we are a community here and that room is a shared space where Ellis from apartment 10B leaves her purple bookmark in the book she's reading to save her place and no one moves it, and Calvin from 3H shares his record player with us and leaves his collection in the lounge for any of us to play," Grandma says. "And I leave my puzzle out . . . I suggest you get used to the way we run things here if you plan on staying long."

Grandma keeps her calm but steady voice when she says, "Now, give me my puzzle." She holds her hand out.

Ms. Sharon walks into the back room of her office and returns with Grandma's puzzle all boxed up. No apology, no nothing.

Grandma yanks the box out of her hands and walks away.

Ms. Norma and Ms. Louise follow her, Ms. Mabel trailing behind on her scooter, mumbling to herself, "Next time I see her walking in the hallway, I'm gonna run her over. I promise you that."

We follow Grandma to the lounge. She sits down, dumps all the pieces out, and starts putting the puzzle together. There are just five pieces snapped in place when she turns and says, "So you all just gonna watch me?"

Ms. Norma sits across from her, starts working.

"But Grandma—"

"You want to help us?" Grandma says. She finds another piece and fits it in its place.

"Ms. Sharon said—"

"Now, which piece do you think goes here?" Grandma says out loud, asking no one in particular.

And for the rest of the afternoon we put the puzzle together. We work on it for two hours, and even though we've made good progress, of course it's not finished because not even five people can put a fifteen-hundred-piece puzzle together in two hours. Grandma walks over to the bookshelf and takes a sheet of paper out of the scrap paper box. She grabs a black marker and writes: DO NOT REMOVE and tapes it on the table.

"Ready for dinner?" she asks.

Everyone says yes, and we all make our way to her apartment. Grandma fries up mackerel patties, and I make the white rice. The kitchen is sizzling and smelling good, and once everything is ready, Grandma calls JT over and we all eat together, having seconds and thirds, and no one brings up Ms. Sharon or the puzzle, and no one seems worried the puzzle might be gone when we go back.

Except me.

All I want to do is go back to the lounge, check on Grandma's puzzle, but it is clear that the group has moved on. First, they are talking about taking the group trip with other Sugar Hill residents to Atlantic City. Ms. Norma says she's only going because of a restaurant she likes there.

And Grandma says, even though she doesn't gamble she'll go since Ms. Mabel and Ms. Louise really want to. Ms. Mabel and Ms. Louise definitely plan on gambling. JT says, "I'll let you ladies have your time and sit that one out." Grandma doesn't seem to mind.

I am proud of myself for not checking my phone this whole time. But now, it is buzzing and I am hoping it is Tye calling to talk, calling to hear my voice. But it's a text from Aunt Ebony to me and Imani asking if we'll be home for dinner. I reply, letting them know I'm having dinner with Grandma. Imani replies: **I'm having dinner with Asher's family.**

This is the first conversation we've technically had since yesterday. I am looking at my phone, double-checking for missed call notifications from Tye when Ms. Mabel blurts out, "So, Nala, did it work? Did using us get you a boyfriend?"

My heart beats faster, but I knew I'd have to have this conversation eventually. "No, actually. I don't think I have a boyfriend anymore. But, but I—I wasn't using any of you. Especially not you, Grandma. I really do enjoy coming here, and I really do love spending time with all of you."

They are all quiet, just waiting for me to say more.

"I'm sorry for lying, though. And I'm sorry if any of you felt hurt."

Grandma says, "So what will you do to make sure you will grow from this?"

"What do you mean?" I ask. "There's nothing I can do . . . other than apologize."

"There's got to be more you can do," she says.

"Well, I can't do anything about Tye. I think he's pretty much done with me. And Ms. Sharon was very clear that I can't do the photo project until winter, so right now, I'm not sure what I can do."

"Hmm," is all Grandma says. And no one else says anything. I am not used to these women and JT being so quiet. They always, always have something to say.

"I'm not like you, Grandma. I can't just go to Ms. Sharon and tell her I am doing it anyway and start painting."

"No one expects that. But you've got to decide who you'll become after this," Grandma says. "For *you*."

I feel like Grandma is talking in some kind of code and I just don't have the energy to figure out what she is trying to tell me, teach me. I just say, *okay*, so that we can move on and talk about something else. But I think Grandma knows that I don't fully understand her. She stands and says, "Well, Nala. I accept your apology. I was disappointed, but I do appreciate you coming here today." She walks into the kitchen, grabs a large knife, and begins to peel the mangoes that are sitting in a ceramic bowl on the counter. "Dessert, anyone?"

We all say yes and fill our bellies with juicy, sweet mangoes.

When I get home, Aunt Ebony and Uncle Randy are sitting on the stoop drinking Red Stripe beers. They say hello, but neither of them push me to talk about Tye and Imani and my lies. I go upstairs to my room, replaying everything that happened today with Grandma, how sure of herself she is and how she refused to back down. How she stood up for herself, for her home. She is absolutely herself at all times. I want to be like that. I stare at myself in the mirror and think about how Grandma told me that I need to figure out how to love myself, how I need to figure out who I'll become after this.

I go to sit on my bed, but it's covered in the stuff from the Inspire Harlem tote bag. I bundle what I don't want in my arms and walk over to the garbage can but then remember to separate the paper from everything else. I'll put what's recyclable in the bin downstairs. The rest, I throw away.

I look again at the Inspire Harlem postcard I pinned on my corkboard. I think about how Grandma said loving yourself is the real revolution. I take out my notebook and make another list.

1. Remember Yourself.
2. Honor Yourself.
3. Critique Yourself.
4. Love Yourself.

This is how I plan to grow.

❧ 22 ❧

Three days have gone by, and I still have not spoken to Imani. Mostly because we haven't been in the same room at the same time. Somehow, we keep missing each other. Okay, not somehow—we keep missing each other because she stays out late with Asher and by the time she comes home I am sleeping. In the mornings, I stay in my room listening to Blue and holding my pee until she leaves (I almost didn't make it to the bathroom in time this morning, so maybe I need to stop this). I haven't been back to see Grandma either. I am still thinking about everything she said, thinking about who I want to be.

The house is quiet, so after I get dressed, I make my way downstairs only to realize Uncle Randy is in the kitchen. He is drinking coffee and reading the paper. "'Morning," he says.

"Good morning." I was going to make breakfast, maybe

boil an egg and make toast, but I'm too embarrassed to be in here with him. I go to the fridge, grab a strawberry yogurt, and head back to my room.

"Before you go, I wanted to talk with you." Uncle Randy closes his paper. I have no choice but to sit with him at the table in the kitchen nook. One side is a bench, the other side, two chairs. I slide in and sit on the bench. I brace myself for what Uncle Randy is going to say. He comes over to the table and sits with me.

"So Liz said we can have the birthday party on the rooftop. She's already reserved it. Imani is going to help pick out food for the evening, and she's helping me pull together a guest list," he says. "Can you work on putting together some kind of special gift?"

I am relieved. "*That's* what you want to talk about?"

Uncle Randy laughs. "What did you think I wanted to talk about?" he asks. And then before I can answer he says, "Oh—that? Not much I can tell you. You already know what you need to do. Imani does too." Uncle Randy takes a long sip of his coffee.

I love Uncle Randy for not making a big deal about any of this. I love him for trusting me to figure it out and fix it on my own.

I eat my yogurt and leave the house, not really having a destination in mind. Just want to get out of the house. If

I'm distracted and walking around, I'm less likely to check my phone to see if Tye has called, or sent a text, or posted on Instagram.

I walk downtown on Frederick Douglass and keep going until I get to 110th. The statue of Frederick Douglass stands tall, and the fountain that sprays out water is on in full force, so little ones are jumping in and out, running around the concrete steps. I cross the street and enter Central Park. I keep walking and walking, trying not to think about Tye or check my phone.

I sit in the park for an hour, just people watching and thinking about the times my mom would bring me here to go to the zoo. Once I'm ready to go home, I walk to the bus stop because I realize I walked a lot farther than I intended to and now I don't want to walk all the way back.

I am sitting at the back of the bus, listening to music through my headphones and minding my own business when out of the corner of my eye, I see someone waving at me. "Excuse me, can I—can I talk to you for a sec?" the boy asks as he steps closer to me. He is talking low and has a gentleness about him. "I like your style," he says.

"Thank you."

I like his too, actually.

"You, uh, you got a boyfriend?"

"I—yes, I do. Well, no. I mean, I don't know."

Nala, really? That's your answer?

"So, if you don't know, I think that means no," the boy says.

And hearing him say that makes my eyes water. "I, um, this is my stop." I stand up and push the tape strip.

"Wait. Hold on. Can I get your number?"

The tears don't wait to fall. "No, I—no." I get off the bus. I decide to go ahead and walk the rest of the way. I am getting used to crying in public. I put my sunglasses on and walk, hiding my red eyes.

I am a block away from home when my phone starts buzzing in my pocket. The first person I think about is the guy on the bus even though I know I didn't give him my number. I don't take it out to see who it is. It's probably Aunt Ebony checking in to ask if I've worked on my essay. I know as soon as I pick up and say hello, she'll detect my tears and want to talk about it, so I just let it go to voice mail.

The afternoon sun is beaming down, and now that I am not in the park anymore under all those trees, I feel the heat even more.

I keep walking and crying and sweating and finally, I am home.

When I get inside, all I want to do is drink a gallon of water and cry.

I don't have a boyfriend anymore.

I am not anyone's girlfriend.

The more I realize it, the harder I cry.

I get a glass of water. My phone buzzes again. A reminder that I didn't answer it before. I don't take it out. I just sit and cry until I have no more tears. I go upstairs, and first, I just sit on my bed and do nothing, but then, I take out my notebook, make more lists.

TIPS FOR SHOWING YOURSELF LOVE

1. Show yourself love by making a playlist that affirms, motivates, and encourages. Music affects my mood, and even though I didn't intend to, starting my day with Blue has been healing and giving me the strength to hold my head up—even though I've messed up. I'm making a playlist with some of my favorite songs, songs that uplift me, songs that remind me I am worthy of love just as I am. First artist on the list will be Blue.

2. Show yourself love by doing what makes you happy. I know I'll have to do some things in life that I don't really love. But there has to be room to squeeze in some fun, some smile-making

moments. For me, it's walking through New York City, people watching and window shopping. For me, it's sharing music and having listening parties with friends, it's spending time with Grandma building puzzles and talking about life. I can do more of this, I need to.

3. Show yourself love by keeping a gratitude journal. I'll need to read it on days when it feels like I have nothing to be grateful for.

I feel my phone vibrating in my pocket again, and then I remember that I never checked to see who was trying to get ahold of me before. I take my phone out, but not in enough time. I missed Sadie's call. I check the rest of my notifications and see that I have a text message. It's from Tye: **Had my phone off for the past few days. Needed to think. Can we talk?**

I don't respond right away. I can't move, can't get my fingers to type anything. I toss the phone back on my bed, pick up the glass of water on my nightstand. I drink the water. Slow. When I swallow the last drop, I pick up my phone, send my reply.

Yes.

23

We agreed to meet at my place.

As soon as I said okay, I regretted it because if this conversation goes bad, I don't want to have to remember it every time I walk up the stoop, every time I open the door. Breakups are better in public spaces, places you don't have to go back to if you don't want to.

Last night, I could hardly sleep thinking about what I needed to say to Tye, wondering what he wanted to say to me. I'm glad we set the time for morning. There's no way I could wait all day to talk with him. It is just before noon and I am sitting on the stoop when I see Tye walking up the block. My heart was beating fast until now. Now it feels stuck, like when someone is holding you up on a see-saw and you have no control. This feels like that.

"Hey," Tye says. He barely looks at me, so I look away from him too.

"Hey."

Tye sits down next to me, but not as close as he normally would. We don't jump in right away, but we don't do pleasantries either. We just sit. A few people walk by, nod or say hello, but mostly, the block is quiet and we are alone.

"I'm sorry, Tye," I finally say. My heart still stuck, still held in suspense. "I want you to know that I never meant to hurt you or make a fool of you. Or—well, I don't know how you're feeling. I just know that I didn't mean to make you feel anything negative."

Tye takes a deep breath but doesn't say anything.

"I . . . when I met you, I was just so impressed by you and I wanted to impress you too. I wanted to be on your level. I just said whatever I thought you'd want to hear because I wanted you to like me."

Tye is still breathing his deep breaths. In, out. He is still not looking at me.

I tell him everything I've lied about, every stretch of the truth. And then I say, "I understand why you don't want to be with me anymore."

"Who said I didn't want to be with you anymore?" Tye says. He looks at me now, and like always his eyes pierce right through me. "I just, I needed time to think. That was a lot."

"Wait. You—you don't want to break up with me?" I ask.

"No. Do you want to break up with me?"

"I thought we were already broken up."

Tye takes my hand. "I mean, I thought about it. I was really upset, Nala. I feel like I don't know you at all. I wanted to talk today, find out what is actually real about you, about us. Did you ever actually have feelings for me?"

"Of course. I, yes. I still do."

Tye looks relieved when I say this. We are quiet again, and this time I don't know what to say to get the conversation going. After a while Tye says, "Well, I do have a lot of questions and there's a lot we need to talk about, but, Nala, spending time with you is good for me. You open me up, have me doing stuff that, I don't know—I guess what I'm trying to say is that I have fun with you. I feel more like myself with you than with anyone else."

I never thought that maybe Tye isn't always being himself, isn't always sure of who he is. I wonder what parts of himself he hides. "You feel more like yourself with me? Who are you when you're with everyone else?"

"I, well, it's just that when I'm with you I feel like I can put my guard down. That I don't have to be perfect."

"Who makes you feel like you have to be perfect?"

"Everyone. My mom, my uncle, my teachers, Ms. Lori." Tye lets out a sigh and says, "I'm a Black boy—there's not a lot of room for error."

"That's a lot of pressure," I say.

"Tell me about it. Pressure to talk right, dress right, get good grades, do the right thing. No mistakes, no second chances." The clouds shift and for a moment there is relief from the sun. "That's why I love spending time with you. I don't feel any pressure with you. I can just be." Tye takes my hand. "I don't want to let that go. I just want to know who you really are."

"That's just it, Tye. I don't know who I really am. I mean, I think I know . . . I'm—I'm learning who I am."

A man walking his dog passes us. I wait until he is far enough away that he can't hear me. I don't want anyone to know this yet, just Tye. I whisper, "I don't think we should be together right now." I expect tears to come when I say this, but they don't. My heart is relaxed, it's off the seesaw, released from suspense. "This isn't because I don't love you, it's because I need to learn how to love myself. For myself."

Part of me is screaming inside, asking what is wrong with me, why am I letting go of someone who cares about me, wants me, forgives me. But I yell back at her, reminding her what Grandma said.

Self-love is radical love.

Self-love is radical love.

Self-love is radical love.

Today, I've started my own revolution.

24

REMEDIES TO A BROKEN HEART

1. Ice cream. Any flavor. In a sugar cone, or waffle
   cone, or cake cone. In a bowl or cup, soft-serve,
   hand-dipped. With pie, or cake, or cookies, or
   fruit, or all by itself. A scoop, two scoops, maybe
   even three—not more than a pint, at least not all
   at once, because even if it heals your heart, it will
   definitely hurt your stomach.

2. Reality TV. Pick your guilty pleasure. Home
   makeover marathons, singing competitions,
   cooking competitions, dating experiments, true
   life crime, behind the scenes with celebrities.
   Sometimes paying attention to someone else's
   drama helps to put your own in perspective.

3. Spa treatment. Okay, "treatment" sounds fancy. All I mean is, I am painting my own nails and giving myself a pedicure. Usually I rush when I do my nails—I hate waiting for them to dry. But today, I've lit a candle, I'm playing music (Blue, of course), and I'm taking my time. After all, a spa treatment should feel like a treat, not a chore.

4. Cry. I don't know why people try not to cry, why we hold it in. I have decided to cry as much and as hard as I need to. Sometimes it is a snotty nose sob, the kind that bellows out, echoing off the high ceilings. An earthquake cry that shakes my insides and makes my shoulders tremble. And sometimes, it comes in silence. Just tears bubbling up in the corners of my eyes, sometimes falling, but sometimes just swaying in the ebb and flow of sorrow. Sometimes the cry comes without tears, comes in the shake of my voice, the hoarseness. Sometimes it comes camouflaged as laughter. (See number 2 to know what I'm laughing about.) I laugh to keep from crying. A belly laugh, even. But still, the tears are there. And the afternoon goes on, crying and laughing, crying and laughing. And

that saying *I laughed so hard I cried* takes on a
whole new meaning.

I get a text from Sadie: **what are you doing?**
Me: **crying.**
Sadie calls me, asks me what's wrong, and when I tell
her she says, "I'm coming over," and hangs up the phone
before I can tell her not to. Knowing Sadie is coming over
makes me get off my bed, wash my face, and go downstairs. My head hurts from all the sobbing, so I don't feel
like doing much but I am glad I will have company. Aunt
Ebony and Uncle Randy are gone for the weekend to the
Poconos, and Imani is with Asher (surprise, surprise).

An hour later, Sadie is at my door, and when she comes
in she doesn't ask me how I am doing or do I want to talk
about it. Instead, she says, "Have you heard Koffee's new
song?" and we spend the rest of the night eating pizza and
listening to music. I start putting a playlist together: Koffee, Shenseea, Masika, Lauryn Hill. Listening to the music
makes us look up videos online, and we dance and we are
singing so loud, dancing so hard, so free.

And then, I hear a noise, see a shadow.

Imani is home.

"You two having a party without me?" she says. It is
not said as a question.

241

Sadie is oblivious. "Hey, girl." She pauses the video. "Where you been?"

"With Asher," Imani says. "You spending the night?"

And that's when I look at the clock, see that it is midnight and I have no idea how all this time passed without me realizing it. Sadie didn't know how late it was either. She grabs her phone, says, "My mom is going to kill me." She calls her mom, explains that she lost track of time, and asks—begs—to spend the night. "I'll come home first thing in the morning." Her face flashes a smile, and so I know her mom said yes. She didn't mention that Aunt Ebony and Uncle Randy aren't here. But they wouldn't care anyway.

I am glad that Sadie is staying over. She doesn't even know it, but she is a buffer between me and Imani. For the first time since our argument at Grandma's, Imani is sitting in my room, actually speaking to me. "What did you do today?" she asks.

I would say nothing, but I am done with lying, so I tell the truth. "I broke up with Tye today."

Imani's eyes fill with shock. "*You* broke up with *him?*"

Sadie gives her a look. "Why you say it like that?"

"Well, I mean, I just assumed he'd be the one who would call things off. I mean, Nala lied, she—"

"I know what she did. But Tye loves her. He chose to forgive her," Sadie says.

"So if he's forgiven you, Nala, why did you break up with him? What was the point of all of this?"

"Why do you care? Isn't this what you wanted—to break us up?"

Sadie stands. "Um, maybe I should leave so you two can have privacy and—"

"Sadie, you don't have to leave," I tell her. Then, I look at Imani and tell her, "Say what you have to say."

Now, Imani gets all quiet and doesn't say anything.

"Imani, I'm embarrassed and ashamed, but I'm not sorry. Not toward you. I don't understand why there's tension between us. I've already talked with Grandma and Tye. I feel like you think I owe you an apology, but I didn't do anything to you."

Imani stands up quick, like a fire is under her. "You did do something to me. First of all, you embarrassed me. I brought you around my friends, and you went out of your way to mock everything we stand for. And every chance you get, you get closer and closer to *my* mother, and now, you've messed with my friend's heart. Get your own life."

Sadie says, "Come on, you two. You're family. Don't do this."

"We need to do this," I say. And then I walk over to

Imani, make sure she is looking at me when I ask her, "Do you want me to move out? You keep bringing up my relationship with Aunt Ebony. Do you want me to leave? Give you back your mother?"

Sadie doesn't let Imani talk. She blurts out, "Imani—don't answer that. You two are emotional right now. Just talk tomorrow . . . don't say anything you'll regret."

Imani and I are standing face-to-face. I am looking at my cousin-sister-friend, waiting for her to tell me she doesn't want me to live with her anymore, that she doesn't want to share her mother, her friends, her life with me. We are a mirror to each other, tears in her eyes, tears in mine. She doesn't answer my question. She takes Sadie's advice, turns around, walks away.

The next morning, Sadie wakes me up with a whisper. "I'm leaving, okay? Gotta get home to watch my little brother." She is standing at the side of my bed, her bag on her shoulder, MetroCard already in her hand.

"Wait, let me walk you out." I slide out of bed, my head still pounding from yesterday's stress. We walk downstairs, and I open the front door for her. "Thanks for coming over," I say.

Sadie gives me a hug. "Text me if you need me later. Hope you and Imani work things out."

I close the door, and instead of going back into my room and hiding till Imani leaves, I go upstairs and knock on her door.

"Come in."

When I open the door, the room is full of sunlight. The glow bounces off Imani's white bedsheets. Everything in her room is in its place. She has never been messy, always all of her seems perfect. I stand at the door, leave it open, and lean against the frame. My arms are folded, even though I don't want to seem guarded. I can't help it. I don't know her answer to my question. I don't know if today I will be packing my bags and going back to my mom's house. And I know technically Aunt Ebony and Uncle Randy have the last say—it is their house after all. But I don't want to be here if Imani doesn't want me here. That feeling is in my chest again, the seesaw feeling. I'm suspended up, up, up. No control over how hard the fall is going to be.

Imani doesn't turn around to face me. She is still in bed, under a thin sheet, lying on her side. Her back is to me. Even though I am the one who's come to her room to talk, she is the one who begins. "I'm sorry, Nala. I said a lot of things last night that I didn't really mean." Imani's voice is always hoarse in the morning. She sounds like she is still half-asleep, I think maybe her eyes are still closed. "I don't want you to leave."

"I know."

Imani turns over, faces me. "I just, I don't know. Since we were babies we've always been compared to each other. Every single thing we do. When it comes to Inspire Harlem, I just want to exist without having to worry about that. And you don't even like hanging with us anyway."

"Well, that's only because when you're with them, you change. And even when you're not with them, sometimes you seem so . . . judgmental."

Imani sits up, cross-legged in her bed, her back against the headboard. "I don't mean to be judgmental. I think I'm just used to being the leader, the one who has to take care of you, show you the way I guess. I mean, that's how it's always been."

"But that's just it, it doesn't need to be like that anymore. I don't need you to speak for me or feel responsible for teaching me. I don't want to be your shadow. I want to stand in my own light." I walk over to Imani's bed and sit on the edge. "And I need to give you and Aunt Ebony time alone, to just hang out without me. I'm sorry if—"

"You have nothing to apologize for, Nala. I need to be home more. That's on me."

We sit for a moment, not knowing what else to say.

Then Imani says, "We don't have to hug now, do we?" and she slides back under her covers, laughing.

I yank the sheet off her, take it with me, and run out of the room. "No," I shout. "And we don't have to say *I love you* either."

You know when someone loves you. You just know.

25

It's just past noon, and the city is a symphony of chaos. Everything is making noise all at once, but somehow there is a calmness to the block I am walking down. Every sound complementing each other, the brakes of the bus, the honking horns, the bounce of the basketball, the slap of the jump rope against concrete. The laughing from the boys standing at the corner cracking jokes and talking big, the delivery guy swerving and zigzagging through traffic dinging his bell to alert people to move out of his way, the woman yelling into her phone like it's a bullhorn, telling all her business.

Before I get to Grandma's, I stop at the ice cream shop to get JT a sundae. I get hot fudge for him and a caramel sundae for me. Grandma has an appointment with her doctor, so I don't have to sneak in the building. When I get to Grandma's, Ms. Sharon is at the front desk as usual. "Ms. June isn't here right now," she tells me.

"I know," I tell her.

I don't explain why I am here. I just go straight to JT's, knock on his door.

When he sees me, he smiles real big. "Miss Nala," he says. "Come on in."

"Hi, JT. I have something for you." I hand him his sundae.

"I've said it before and I'll say it again, you are too kind. Too kind." He sits at the dining room table, and I sit with him. We start eating our ice cream, and like always, he asks me, "So what's on your mind?"

This time I have an answer.

"Everything."

JT laughs. "Miss Nala, you are one of extremes. I ask you what's on your mind one day, you answer *nothing*. I ask you the next day, you tell me *everything*."

"Okay, well, not everything." I laugh a little. JT is eating his ice cream slow, but I am almost finished with mine. "I've been thinking a lot about Tye and how I really messed things up."

"He's having a hard time forgiving you?"

"No, actually. He's—he wants to work things out. I'm the one who broke up with him."

JT puts his spoon down. "So, you're having a hard time forgiving yourself?"

I don't have an answer for that.

JT tells me, "Don't get me wrong. There's no excuse for what you did. But you apologized, right?"

"Yes."

"Well, you've got to let people forgive you. Sounds like that young man—what's his name?"

"Tye."

"Yes, right. Sounds like Tye is trying to give you what you asked for. You want forgiveness, you've got to receive it. Don't do you no good to punish yourself. Just be a better person today, tomorrow." JT scrapes the last little bit of ice cream from his cup.

"JT, you think Grandma will be angry at us if she finds out I've been bringing you ice cream?"

"Oh, Miss Nala. I reckon she already knows."

JT is probably right.

3 THINGS I NEED TO FORGIVE MYSELF FOR

1. For being just as judgmental as the people who have judged me.

2. For competing with other girls instead of complimenting them.

3. For pretending to be anyone other than the perfectly imperfect person I am.

26

August has come with a vengeance. It is humid and sticky, and I've only walked one block and already I want to change my clothes. I hate to sweat. I hate the way it oozes down my forehead. I hate how no matter how much I wipe it away, it comes back. I hate the way my thick legs rub together under my skirt, how when I lift my arms there are sweat stamps on my shirt. Aunt Ebony said nobody in their right mind would go out in all this heat, but I have to get her birthday gift, so I give an excuse about needing to get something from Sadie and head out into the furnace.

I decided to get a photo album made. Each family member gets their own page and has written a message or memory to Aunt Ebony with a photo on the page. I did the layout online, and now it's ready for pickup. I hope it turns out the way I envision it, and I hope Aunt Ebony likes it. It's the only thing I could think of that's a unique gift, something she doesn't have. I got the idea because I know for her class, she always gives a photo to each of her students on the last day of school with a note on the back. I think people give the type of gifts they want to receive, so maybe she'd like some version of that. Uncle Randy and Imani think it's a great idea.

On my way to the bus stop, I go to the store and buy two bottled waters so I can stay hydrated while I'm out. I cross the street after I leave the store and wait at the bus stop under a tree. It gives a little bit of shade, but I am still hot, still sweaty. I have headphones in my ears, so I don't hear any of the street commotion, but I hear someone calling my name. I pull the left pod out of my ear and turn around.

It's Tye.

My heart tumbles, like a person falling down stairs. *Bump, bump, bump.* I feel it all out of sorts inside me. My mind is flooded with so many thoughts. Number one—of all the days to see Tye, why right now when I am a hot, sweaty mess? And number two—how is it that he looks even better than the last time I saw him? I am more and more anxious the closer he gets.

Tye gives me a shy smile, like he doesn't know me (and does he?). "Hey, Nala."

"Hey."

We don't know what to say to each other, and I'm sure the woman standing next to me is wondering what our story is. I see her trying not to be nosy, but she can't help it. That's how it is in New York. Everyone hears everything, sees everything even if they don't want to.

"So, what are you up to today?" I ask.

"Heading to the store. Need to get a few things for my mom. I just, I, uh, I saw you from across the street, so I wanted to say hello. So, uh, yeah—hi."

"Hi." I have to push the word out because really what I want to say is, *can we talk?* and *do you miss me as much as I miss you?*

The bus turns the corner, and the not-trying-to-be-nosy woman walks to the curb. I stand behind her. Once the bus pulls over, I pull my MetroCard out. "See you around," I say.

"Yeah, see you."

But when?

THINGS I MISS ABOUT TYE

1. His smile. There is always a story behind his
   smile, a poem hiding there so gentle, subtle. How
   his laugh asks questions, like, are you serious?
   Are you sure? We have had whole conversations

with raised eyebrows, smirks, reluctant grins. We don't always need words to communicate.

2. His hands. The way they reach out for me when we are walking side by side, how they reach out for me when we're at the edge of the sidewalk, urging me not to cross yet, to just stand still with him while everyone else is moving. How his fingers trace the outline of my face, write invisible words onto my skin. His hands that have held me while watching the sun set, watching movies, people watching. Always his arms are some type of shelter, some type of safe place where I feel like nothing can touch me, us.

3. His lips. The kisses, yes, but also the way they are bridges to the words that come out of him, the way he moves them gently to say, *I think I'm falling in love with you.* The way they tense up when he's talking about his dad. His lips that have pressed against mine, over and over again, over and over again.

I take the bus to the print shop so I can pick up Aunt Ebony's gift. She is the only person I would be out in this heat for. I get to the store and give the man at the counter my name. He disappears for a bit and then comes back with the most beautiful photo album I've ever seen. The cover is canvas, and a picture of the whole family is on the cover. Inside, page after page is filled with memories that we can now hold in our hands, not just see on a computer screen. I know she's going to love this. After I look through the album, the man at the counter wraps it for me, puts it in a bag, and slides in several coupons. "A little incentive for you to come back," he says. "I'm giving you special discounts on albums and individual prints as well."

"Thank you."

"Have a nice day. And come back to see us."

"I will."

When I get home, I hide the album in the back of my bedroom closet. I sit on my bed for a while, just trying to cool off from being outside in all that heat. I lie down on my back, across my bed looking up at the ceiling.

I saw Tye today.

I can't get him off my mind.

I pick up my phone, think about calling him. No, maybe a text. Maybe I should reach out and tell him how nice it was to see him today, tell him how much I miss him. I sit up and type a few messages but delete them all.

Then, I get my notebook, work on me instead.

GRATITUDE LIST

1. I am grateful for Sadie because she sees me, feels me, doesn't judge me.

2. I am grateful for Grandma's friends at Sugar Hill. The way they make me laugh, think. How JT is like a grandfather, how the women are bonus grandmothers to me. How we are all family.

3. I am grateful for Aunt Liz for being the example of independence, style, and excellence.

4. I am grateful for Blue for making music that heals my heart.

27

BLUE PLAYLIST, TRACK 8

Missing You Interlude

The sun is setting.
It reminds me of your smile.
How it is always so stunning
but never the same twice.
How even as I watch it fade away,
still I am not ready to see it go.

Imani tells me that Inspire Harlem is having an end-of-summer gathering for family and friends. I really don't want to go because I know Tye will be there. And his mom. And Toya will be there. And everyone else who knows that I lied and who saw me on stage making a fool of myself reciting song lyrics. So yeah, I don't really want to go but part of me does. I want to go because Imani is getting an award and I know it will mean a lot to her if I'm there.

I haven't decided yet. But what I did decide to do is donate all those party supplies I bought with Tye. Ms. Lori was so happy to have them. "Just in time," she said to thank me. "We'll use these for decorations at the ceremony."

I kind of want to go just to see how they'll use the decorations.

I don't have much longer to decide because today's the day. Right now, I am hanging out with Aunt Ebony, helping her prep for the school year. Summer is almost gone. Just a few more weeks and we'll be back to our fall and winter routine. We are in the family den, and I am working on posters and charts that Aunt Ebony will laminate later and hang in her classroom.

Imani comes in the room, takes the ironing board out of the closet, and says, "Mom, the potluck is in an hour— you didn't forget, did you?"

"Of course not. I'll be ready. Your dad will be home soon, and we'll all walk over together."

Imani looks at me. "Are you sure you don't want to come to the potluck?" She is standing at the ironing board with scissors in her hand, cutting an old shirt into a crop top to wear with a new long, flowing skirt she bought last week.

This is an event for family, and I am her cousin-sister-friend, so I should be there. I finish helping Aunt Ebony and get up and head to my room to change into something more presentable and say to Imani, "Don't leave without me."

The potluck is happening at the Countee Cullen Library. It looks so different from the night of the talent show. The lights are bright, and there are long tables on two sides of the room covered with all the food families have brought. In the middle of the room are round tables, covered with tablecloths with small succulent plants in the middle as centerpieces. Aunt Ebony brought drinks and chips and dip, said it was too hot to cook. We get there just as it's starting. Ms. Lori is at the front of the room. "Can I get everyone's attention, please? Everyone, can I get your attention?" A hush moves through the crowd, and once it is quiet, Ms. Lori says, "I just wanted to welcome you all to our first—and hopefully annual—Inspire Harlem family potluck. We're here today to connect, eat some good food, and honor our teen community leaders. Please feel free to help yourselves to the delicious feast that's been prepared, and we'll get started with the awards ceremony shortly."

I'm not sure if we should clap or not—a few people

offer applause but most of us just start heading to the food tables. I survey the crowd to see if Tye is here yet. He is not.

But Toya is.

I see her in line making her plate, talking with Lynn, who is pouring the pineapple juice Aunt Ebony brought into a cup. I don't realize that I am actually staring at them, and so when Toya waves, I have to wave back because I can't pretend I don't see her. They walk over to me, and Toya says, "I didn't know you were coming."

Like I would have told her.

"Yeah, wanted to come support Imani."

Toya stands there as if she expects me to say more. Then, I see Sadie walking over, a big smile on her face. "Hey, girl," she says as she wraps her arms around me. "My mom and dad are over there with your family, you coming?" She points across the room to Aunt Ebony and Uncle Randy. We fix our plates and head over there, waving bye to Toya and Lynn. Just as I am walking over to get a seat, I see Tye come in. He is with his mom, and he is looking across the room, his eyes searching. Is he looking for me? Is he hoping I'm here . . . hoping I'm not here? My heart aches, and even though this food looks so good, I don't want to eat it anymore.

He doesn't see me.

I sit down, try to act normal when Sadie's mom asks how I'm doing. I don't move out of this seat all afternoon. Sadie has gone back for seconds and brought me something to drink. She hasn't asked why I'm not mingling. She knows.

The program starts, and it is moving along pretty quickly, no long speeches or special performances. Just Ms. Lori bringing up each Inspire Harlem teen one by one so they can receive their certificate while she says some nice words about them. For Imani, she says, "This young lady is beyond dedicated. She is the first to arrive, the last to leave, and she is willing to take the lead or work behind the scenes." We all clap as Imani takes the certificate. I snap a photo, but it probably won't look too good because I have to zoom in so much, I am sure it is blurry and pixelated.

Then, Ms. Lori says, "Now this next person is the newest member of Inspire Harlem, and I just can't see our community without him. He's a compassionate and patient individual. And what I love most is that he leads by example. Mr. Tye Brown, please come to the stage."

We all clap, and when Tye makes it to the stage, he hugs Ms. Lori, then looks out into the audience, and that's when our eyes connect. He sees me, and he doesn't look away.

Once the potluck is over, everyone stands around

talking and no one is leaving even though the custodial staff have come and started cleaning. Tye and his mother are talking with Asher's family, who are just a table away. It's so hard to be this close to him without speaking to him, without reaching out to hug him. I go outside, stand against the brick wall, and pretend to be looking for something on my phone. And then I hear him; he must have followed me out here.

"I miss you," he says.

I turn around, and he is right there, so close I can feel the heat from his body. "I miss you too."

"You do?"

"Of course. Why do you sound surprised?"

"Well, I mean, you're the one who broke up with me."

Is this his way of saying he'd take me back?

I don't get to ask him because Ms. Brown comes out, carrying a to-go container, and says, "Come on, Tye." She looks at me without emotion and says, "Hi, Nala."

I can barely get a hello out. I'm not sure either of them hear me say it as they walk away.

MORE THINGS I MISS ABOUT TYE

1. That I can't call him whenever something good is on TV that I know he would want to watch too.

2. That we don't text each other good morning or heart emojis or see you tomorrows anymore. No one is checking on me just to say hello, just to say *hey, I'm thinking of you.*

3. That I don't have anyone to roam New York City with. Sure, I can explore by myself or with Sadie, but sometimes—most times—I want him with me to see the street performers at Union Square, to witness the wild happenings on the subway, to share a too-big pizza slice, to grab a table at the crowded coffee shop while I order at the counter. Two is better than one sometimes. Most times.

28

Aunt Ebony invited me and Imani out for lunch, but I told them I think she should have a day with just Imani. Once they both leave, I go over to Grandma's, and I realize that JT is right about Grandma. She knows that I bring him an ice cream sundae every now and then, but she isn't saying anything. Today, when I get to her place, she absolutely sees me with the sundaes, getting on the elevator. "Going to visit JT?" she asks.

"Yes. I was going to call you when we're done talking."

"Okay. I'll be in the lounge." I can't believe that Grandma doesn't fuss at me or come with me. She just walks away and acts like it doesn't bother her at all. She doesn't even get on me for hiding this from her.

I knock on JT's door, and when he opens it, he says what he always says, "Nala, my dear, you are too kind. Too kind."

We sit and eat our ice cream like we always do, but

today, JT doesn't ask me any questions. He doesn't pry about Tye or ask me about college. After a while, I say to him, "Everything okay?"

He nods.

"You seem quiet today," I tell him.

"Just waiting on you," he says.

Waiting on me?

JT chuckles. "I thought we had our routine down, Nala. You know the drill. What's on your mind?"

I guess I just needed him to ask. I tell JT, "I need to figure out what I'm going to do for college."

"Tell me more," JT says.

"I need to write my personal essay, but I don't know what to write about. I hardly even know what I want to study in college."

JT says, "You don't have to know right now."

"Yes, I do. Aunt Ebony keeps asking me about the essay, and pretty soon she's going to want to read it but I haven't even started yet."

"Maybe that's the problem." JT gets up and throws his ice cream cup away. "Maybe you are writing it for your aunt Ebony and not for yourself."

Now JT sounds like Grandma. What is it with all this talk about doing things for myself? How do you know if you're doing something for yourself or someone else?

"Just write," JT says. "Just write as if no one is going to read it. Write as if you're telling yourself what you need to know."

We spend the rest of the afternoon helping Grandma with her puzzle. Grandma gives me the honor of snapping the last piece in. It's a beautiful scene. Maybe a summer afternoon. Women are sitting on the porch with the backdrop of clothes hanging on the clothesline. There's a woman holding a baby, a woman holding a cat, and children hanging on the banister, all listening to the men who are scattered around the yard playing instruments—a washboard, a bucket, a banjo, and a guitar. Even animals have gathered to listen to the jam session.

"I'll leave it here for a day or two and then start on my next one."

"You're not going to keep it here longer?" I ask. "After all the work we did."

"It's not meant to last forever," Grandma says.

We go back to her apartment, and even though I am not hungry, Grandma makes fried plantains for us to eat. I don't think I've ever come over without her feeding me. I sit on the sofa, and it just feels good to be together, Grandma in the kitchen, no words being spoken, just the two of us hanging out. It reminds me of when I was little and I'd sit on her living room floor, coloring book and crayons spread out, making something while she was in the kitchen cooking up something. I look at Grandma's Bible, see which passage it's open to today, have my three-minute church service. It's placed on 1 Corinthians 13. I start reading.

> Love is patient, love is kind. It does not envy, it does not boast, it is not proud. It does not dishonor others, it is not self-seeking, it is not easily angered, it keeps no record of wrongs. Love does not delight in evil but rejoices with the truth. It always protects, always trusts, always hopes, always perseveres. . . . And now these three remain: faith, hope and love. But the greatest of these is love.

I take a photo of the thin paper. I'll copy these words in my notebook. How is it that these words have existed for so long and I have never heard them? How is it that these words are easy to say, easy to believe in, but so hard to actually do?

"You ready to eat?" Grandma says.

She fixes a plate for me, and we sit at the dining room table and eat. When we are finished, I promise to come back in two days and work on the next puzzle. I hug

Grandma, and as I am walking out of the door, I tell her, "Imani said she's coming over with me next time."

"I'd like that," Grandma says. "I'd really like that."

After leaving Grandma's, I make my way to the library, and as soon as I get inside I get to work on my personal essay. I don't know what I want it to be about, but I take JT's advice. First, I look through my lists and think about all that happened this summer. My lists are all over the place, and a lot of the bullet points I would never share with a panel of strangers who are deciding my educational future, but finally I feel like I'm onto something when I decide to write about what I've learned this summer, all the things I am learning. I look through my notebook and see all the lists I wrote about Tye, about loving him. I only have a few pages left. I turn to a blank page, start another list.

3 THINGS I LOVE ABOUT MYSELF

1. My hair. After experimenting with different styles, I've come to love it for the many ways it can transform, for the story it is always telling.

2. My skin. It is dark brown and looks good in yellow and green and any shade of blue and also

white and also gray, and its scars heal like no pain ever happened, and it glistens under the sun, and in the winter it soaks up shea butter and cocoa butter, and this summer, this summer it soaked up kisses, so many kisses imprinted in this skin of mine.

3. My mind. It is its own. Even though sometimes it is tempted to change, falter. Deep down it is sure, made up, full of ideas and thoughts and sweet memories and an imagination that built faraway places when I was a child, places I transformed into playlands: under tables, in the back seat of the car, on fire escapes and stoops. My mind. It is strong and holds all of who I am. It is still forming and growing and in so many ways, still the same. My mind. It is expansive, and there is so much room to fill, so much more to know.

29

I am setting up for Aunt Ebony's party, lighting the tea lights in the center of the table. Aunt Liz and Imani are arranging the flowers and decorating the space. Uncle Randy has hung white Christmas lights above our heads in a crisscross pattern. It feels like the sky has dropped down, that the stars are hanging so low I can touch them. Aunt Ebony's photo album is on the gift table with a wrapped box from Uncle Randy. The box is huge, but when I move it to make room for the cake, I realize it is not heavy at all. I wonder what he's up to.

The elevator dings, and that is the beginning of guests arriving. There are two teachers who work with Aunt Ebony, a few friends she's had since she moved to New York, and of course Grandma. JT is with her, and everyone is acting like this isn't a big deal, but it definitely is a big deal. Asher and his parents are here too. And I think about

Tye even more when I see them. He would've come tonight if we were still dating. I think Uncle Randy would like him.

The only person we are missing is my mom.

Aunt Liz asks about her. "She's coming, right?"

"She's always late, you know that."

Aunt Liz sighs. "That girl." She checks her phone for the time. "I hope she gets here before Ebony. Randy will be here any minute."

Aunt Liz turns on some music—a mix of old-school R&B songs that Aunt Ebony loves and some reggae classics. Just as I light the last candle, Imani shouts, "My dad just sent me a text. They're on their way up."

Grandma says, "She's knows about this right? We aren't yelling surprise, are we?"

"She knows. He just wanted to make sure everything was set up."

Just then the elevator dings again and Aunt Ebony walks onto the deck. Her face lights up when she sees us all gathered and waiting for her. We all shout out, "Happy Birthday!" and walk over to give her a hug.

The dinner is formal, because Aunt Liz would not have it any other way. There are servers, and everything comes out looking like it was made by a top chef. We are just midway through the main entrée when finally my mom comes. "Sorry, sorry, sorry," she says as soon as she steps off the elevator. She walks over to Aunt Ebony first, gives her a side hug and kisses her on her cheek. "Happy birthday, Eb. Girl, you looking good. You know what they say, Black don't crack." Mom looks the table over and realizes there are assigned seats. Her name is at the seat next to mine. "Okay, Liz. I see you. Doing it up for your sister, huh? This is fabulous."

Mom sits down beside me. "Hey, Nala. You look nice."

"Thank you."

For the rest of the dinner Mom dominates the conversation, telling stories about Aunt Ebony and Aunt Liz and how it was growing up with all girls in the house. I am laughing trying to imagine them as teenagers coming from Jamaica to live in the States, how it must have been hard for them to leave their friends.

Everyone is finished with their dinner, so the servers come and take our plates. Dessert is buffet style because there are so many choices—all sweets that Aunt Ebony loves. Before we can dig in, the server makes an announcement so everyone knows what our options are. "For the birthday girl we've prepared an array of Jamaican sweet treats," he says. "We have coconut drops, which are made from coconut meat, ginger, and brown sugar. We also have mango cheesecake and sweet potato pudding. And because we know this is the birthday girl's favorite, we have banana spice cupcakes. Pick your pleasure and enjoy."

As we all stand and make our way to the dessert table, Mom whispers to me, "So who is he? Nobody told me Momma has a new boo." She is pointing at JT.

"*Mom.*"

"Everybody finding love around here, huh? Even Momma? Hopefully me, you, and Liz will be next."

Mom doesn't know that I actually have found love. I just haven't told her because we never talk about these things. I tell her, "Well, I kind of found it, but let it go."

"Let it go?" Mom picks up a banana spice cupcake and a coconut drop.

"It's a long story, but basically, I just need to learn who I am and how to love myself."

"Well, I don't know the whole story, but does it have to be one or the other?" Mom licks a dollop of cream cheese frosting and waits for me to pick my dessert. I get the mango cheesecake. "Sounds like you gotta get good at doing both. Loving yourself enough not to get lost in him and loving him enough to give him the best of who you are."

There are pockets of people spread out on the rooftop. Some went back to the table, some are sitting in the lawn chairs, or standing along the railing looking down at

Harlem, watching people and cars move from one place to the next. Mom and I feast on our sugar, standing side by side, where we always stand when we're up here. "That chef put his foot in these drops," Mom says.

"And this cheesecake too."

We are eating our last bites when Mom says, "You don't strike me as a girl who doesn't know who she is. You just need to be confident in who you know you are."

We haven't even been home that long, and already we are reminiscing about the party like it happened years ago. "And did you see the way JT was so loving toward Mom?" Aunt Ebony asks.

Uncle Randy nods. "He's good for her." He finishes unpacking the leftovers and puts everything in the fridge. Except the drops. Aunt Ebony has made tea, and we are all gathered in the kitchen eating the rest of the drops and drinking Earl Grey.

"Mom, you have to open your gifts." Imani brings our gifts over to her. "This is from me, this one is from Nala, and this is from Dad."

"I thought my gift was the party," Aunt Ebony says. "This is too much." She reaches for the gift from Imani first. It's a metallic gold envelope with *Mom* written in cursive writing. She carefully opens the flap and slides out a thick card. A small square-shaped paper falls out of the card. She reads it to herself, then says, "Oh my—thanks, Imani. A gift card for a mani and pedi. You girls will have to come with me. We'll have a back-to-school spa day." She kisses Imani on the cheek. "Thanks, love."

"You're welcome."

Uncle Randy says, "Open mine next." He picks up his box, acting like it is the heaviest thing.

When he gives it to Aunt Ebony, she starts laughing. "Is anything in here?" She takes the lid off the box and pulls out an envelope. She opens it and reads the card out loud. "A weekend stay in Cape Cod," Aunt Ebony says. "Yes, please. When are we going?"

"Whenever you want to. Up to you."

"I might start packing tonight." Aunt Ebony kisses Uncle Randy on the lips.

When Aunt Ebony picks up my gift, I tell her, "This is kind of from everyone."

And Imani says, "But it was all her idea and she put it together."

As soon as she opens it, she gives me the tightest hug. "This is . . . oh my goodness." She flips through the pages of the photo album and takes in each photo like she is seeing them for the first time. A few of them, she touches and traces with the tip of her finger. "I haven't had actual printed photos in years," she says. "And look at these hand-written notes throughout the album. The absolute best." Aunt Ebony goes on and on about the photo album for the rest of the night, and I am so glad she doesn't think it's too corny.

Imani and I head upstairs—Imani already on her phone texting Asher even though they just saw each other. On my way to my room I hear Aunt Ebony say, "Today was perfect. And that album. It's literally holding memo-ries in your hand. It's the little things."

It's the little things.

I get to thinking that I know exactly what I want to do with all those frames that have just been sitting in my closet. I can't even go to bed, I'm so motivated to start. I get my phone out, make a folder that says Legacy Project, and go through my phone checking photos from this summer that will be added to the folder. Some of the photos make me smile, like the before and after pictures Sadie and I took with my hair a dripping storm cloud. And then there are the ones from the street ball tournament, and JT and Grandma, and so many of me and Tye. I won't get them all, but I do want to print some of them. I take out the frames and look at the different sizes I have. I decide which photo will go in each frame and upload the photos that I want to print into my online account. I lose track of time resizing the images and adjusting the colors before I finally place the order.

It's the little things.

I think about this while falling asleep. I don't need to do a big photo project at Grandma's residence to make an impact. If I'm going to be true to myself, then being me is all about doing the little things, every day, just because.

30

BLUE PLAYLIST, TRACK 13

All I Need

Hook
Today I am possible.
I have survived and will survive.
And all that is coming is already mine.

Chorus
Not waiting on someone to want me, need me.
No fairy-tale dreams of what my life might be.
I love me.
Right now.
Right now.
I love me.

Verse 1

And even with all my flaws, I am enough.

And I have failed, but I am not a failure.

And love is patient and love is kind and love is not
just for me to give away.

Keep some for myself.

Chorus

Not waiting on someone to want me, need me.

No fairy-tale dreams of what my life might be.

I love me.

Right now.

Right now.

I love me.

Verse 2

And I have peace in knowing

that if something more never comes,

I already have what I need.

Because what I need is me.

There is no way I can be better for anyone else

if I'm not good to me. I gotta be good to me.

Hook

Today I am possible.

I have survived and will survive.

And all that is coming is already mine.

I've been taking out my braids for the last two days, a section at a time, so I don't have to sit for hours. When I finish unbraiding the last section of my hair, I comb through it and wash it. The shower water is warm, and the shampoo foams in my hands, thick like whipped cream. The added hair made my hair sturdy, made me look regal, strong. Now that my own hair is in my hands, nothing added, I feel its softness, feel the coils twisting and tangling around my fingers. I wash and condition and rinse my hair, listening to Blue, letting her words wash over me, cleanse me. And I start singing. I match her voice, hitting every run, every ad lib, and we sing together, like her words are my words. I get out of the shower, dry off, and when I bring the towel to my face, I exhale into the terry cloth and tears pour out of me.

I let out every single one.

And when the next track comes on, I just stand in the full-length mirror and look at myself. My tears all dried up, my heartbeat steady.

And then the next song comes, and I dance. Just me with Blue, here in the bathroom, my hair and body all natural, all mine. Every coil, and roll, and scar. I move my body and sing loud and I don't know if I sound good or not, but it doesn't matter.

Good thing it's just me at home this morning.

I get dressed, take out the blow-dryer, and dry my hair. This is always the worst part. My long, thick hair takes forever to dry, and my arms always ache afterward from all the uncomfortable positions I put them in. Finally, my hair is dry and ready to be straightened. The flat iron is warm, so I pick it up, get started.

I think of the styles I have tried this summer, how at first these new styles—and even the head wrap—were just me trying to fit in, cover something up, prove something. But truth is, I like my hair all kinds of ways. I've made an appointment with Sadie, and she'll hook me up with a new braided style before school starts. She'll add color next time and make the braids thin and extra long. And it will be because I want it, because it looks good on me, and not for any other reason.

It is already two o'clock in the afternoon, and all I've done today is my hair. My cell phone rings, and when I pick it up, I see the photo of me and Mom on the screen. I am five years old in the picture, and we are dressed in the same color—purple. I answer the phone, and Mom starts going on and on about all the back-to-school sales happening and how she wants to take me shopping for school clothes. I tell her I already ordered most of the clothes I need. "There are more stylish plus-size options online," I say.

"Well, you need pencils and paper and whatnot, don't you? At least let me get you some school supplies." This is Mom's way of saying she wants to spend time with me, so I say yes, because I want to see her too.

We meet at Staples, and after filling the handheld basket with notebooks, folders, and gel pens, we wait in a too-long line. I look over everything in the basket and think maybe I should put the decorative folders back. I was going to get the ones that were on sale, but Mom said those were too plain and to go for the ones I really wanted. They cost more because they have an assortment of prints and look nicer than the plain ones. As we wait in line, Mom turns to me and says, "I can't believe you are going to be a senior." She looks me over, taking all of me in. "You are not my baby girl anymore . . . wow."

"They grow up fast, don't they?" a woman behind us says. "Those are mine over there. Thirteen already. Where does the time go?" She points to twin boys who are in the electronic section.

It's our turn to step up to the cashier. I put everything on the counter, and the woman rings them up. When she says the total, Mom digs through her wallet. "Um. But I thought these were on sale." She picks up the packs of pens.

"No, those aren't on sale, ma'am."

"Oh, um . . . and the paper? Isn't the paper on sale?"

"Yes, but you have to buy two in order to get the third pack free."

"Mom, it's okay. I can pay for it. Aunt Ebony gave me—"

"It's fine," Mom says. "I—I got it. Just. Give me a minute." Mom goes into another section of her purse and pulls out a twenty-dollar bill, then she goes back to her wallet and pulls out a credit card. "Can I split the bill and pay for these with this and the rest on the card?"

"Sure. I'll just have to ring it up separately."

"Mom, I have—"

"Nala, it's fine."

Mom pays, twice, and hands the tote bags to me.

When we are out of the store and outside again, I thank her, but I am not sure if she heard me because of all the noise, so I repeat myself, "Thank you, Mom."

"Of course," she says. "You're welcome."

We walk on Lenox Avenue, heading to Aunt Ebony's. Mom is still reminiscing and talking about how she can't believe I am graduating soon. We swap our *remember whens* back and forth, reminding each other of how things used to be. Then Mom says, "And remember how much you loved roller skating?"

"I still do," I tell her. And then I get an idea. "We should go—me, you, Imani, and Aunt Ebony, like old times."

"Oh, that would be so fun," Mom says. "Or should I say, that would be so funny—I haven't skated in years. I'm too old to move like I used to. But I'll go. See what I'm working with."

"Thursday night is family night. Free admission, half off skate rentals." I say this so she knows it's affordable, so she doesn't worry about having the money to go.

Mom doesn't hesitate to ask Aunt Ebony. She sends her a text, and my phone vibrates because she included me on the thread too, and I see Imani's name. My phone buzzes again. Imani is the first to reply, saying, **Yes, I'm in.** And then Aunt Ebony says, **Can't wait. This will be so fun.**

"Well, looks like it's a date," Mom says. "This Thursday." Mom puts her phone back in her purse, and she is smiling so hard, so real. I haven't seen her like this in a long, long while.

31

The next morning, I leave the house early so I can make sure I am at the photo shop right when it opens. Harlem is quiet today and it's bright, but it's not hot yet. Grandma always says it's best to run errands before noon to avoid the afternoon heat. Grandma is never wrong.

I am the second customer in the store. I get in line at the counter and pull out my phone so I can give my order number. The man remembers me and smiles. "You came back to see us." He says "us" even though every time I've been here, he is the only one working. He gives me two envelopes because there are different sizes, and I can't wait to see them. I open the first envelope, pulling the glued-down flap. I open it and step aside to look through the photographs. They are perfect, and I feel like I am holding all the people I love and care about in the palm of my hand.

Once I am home, I take over the dining room table and

lay out all the photos and start framing them. Seeing summer laid out before me I write a simple note to each person I want to give a photo to. I don't know when I'll give them all out, but it's nice to have these gifts ready, these moments of summer forever frozen in time. Without even intending to, I take the photo of me and Tye, put it in one of the gift bags left over from Aunt Ebony's party, and head out the door.

I walk to Tye's place, and once I get there, I am stuck outside like the cement is quicksand. People keep passing me going in and out of the gate. A man sees me and says, "Left your key card? Need me to buzz you in?" I stutter out *no thank you* and keep standing there. I give myself a pep talk. The last time I saw Tye, he said I didn't have to miss him; he basically invited me to make the first move. *Come on, Nala. Just push the buzzer and see if he's home.* I think maybe I should text first. Let him know I am standing out front. I take a few steps to my right and get out of the way. I grab my phone, and just as I am about to text Tye, I hear his voice behind me. "Nala?" I turn around. He has his key card in his hand, holds it up to the sensor, and holds the gate open for me. "What are you doing here?" he asks.

"I—I came to see you."

We walk over to the courtyard instead of going inside his building. At least there's shade to sit in. I sit on one of the benches. Tye doesn't wait for me to begin. "What's up?" he says.

"I'm really sorry, Tye."

He sits down next to me.

"I know I've said this already, but really, I'm sorry. And I do miss you. I just needed a moment. I needed to figure things out. I didn't know myself anymore, and, well, I'm still figuring things out, but I know that doesn't mean that we still can't be in each other's lives . . . I mean, if you still want me in your life."

He doesn't say anything right away, and I start wondering if maybe I've said too much. Or maybe I haven't said enough.

"I still don't know why you did all of this. I mean, why did you think you needed to make up all that stuff?"

"You seemed so perfect. The vibrant, volunteering vegetarian who knows exactly what he wants to do in college, after college. I just didn't think you'd like a girl like me. I mean, do you know how much I love bacon?"

Tye laughs a gut-wrenching laugh, and it feels so good to be with him and his smile. "I love bacon too," he says. "It's what I miss the most." Then, Tye gets serious and says, "Actually, I need to apologize to you."

"For what?"

"For not putting as much attention into *you* as I did

into what you were doing. You're a person, and who you are is just as important. I care about you, not just what you do," Tye says. "Nala, spending time with you is what made this summer so special. Talking with you and getting to know you as a person was way more interesting than talking about the photo project."

When he brings up the photo project, I go into my bag and pull out the framed picture. "So, about that," I say. "This is actually why I came over. I wanted to give something to you." I hand the photo to Tye. "I figured out what to do with all those frames."

He smiles that gorgeous smile and says, "Thank you." He just keeps staring at it, and then looks back at me. "I gotta step my gift-giving up. I'm sorry for giving you things I thought you needed to have, instead of things you wanted."

"Apology accepted. I will put both to use, though. I promise," I say.

Tye puts the photo back in the gift bag. "So, what's the occasion?"

"The occasion?"

"For the gift."

"Because this summer something special happened. Even if it was a bit muddled. And I don't want us to forget it."

Tye looks at the photo again, then says, "This has been the best summer ever. I can't believe it's over next week."

"Me too," I say. I don't know how being back in school will change my relationship with Tye. I know we will both be occupied with senior-everything. We don't even go to the same high school, so it's not like we'll conveniently see each other every day. If we're going to stay in each other's lives, it will have to be on purpose, intentional.

Tye asks, "So, what does this mean—you came over to give me this photo. Is that all?"

"I don't want that to be all," I say. "I kind of feel like we need to start over," I tell him. "I mean, I guess what I'm saying is, I want to start over."

"Yeah, me too."

We sit for a while, and now more people are coming out to sit and play in the courtyard. A siren wails in the background, and three children are splashing in the water fountain giggling and chasing one another. There's a woman walking by pushing a stroller and an elderly man walking with a cane, slowly but surely.

August is ending, and this time next week I'll be sitting in a classroom with a teacher saying something about senior year being an important year, a year for making memories and treasuring every moment because this is it, *real life* is about to begin.

"So how do we start over?" I ask.

Tye says, "Tell me something about you that I don't know."

And we begin again.

A NOTE ABOUT THE SONG LYRICS

Music is such a big part of my life. Music comforts, guides, heals. I almost always have music on in my home. I love how music shifts a mood, creates an atmosphere. And there's nothing like that *amen* moment when a lyric speaks to my heart and says for me what I couldn't put into words but what I feel so, so deeply. I wanted Nala to have that experience. Nala can't always find the words she wants to say, but when she's listening to the singer Blue, she feels validated, heard. Music is a friend to Nala, speaking to her (and for her) and encouraging her to be her best self.

I created the character Blue with the vibe of Lauryn Hill and Koffee in mind, mixed with a little bit of Lizzo and Beyoncé too. All the lyrics are inspired by the poetic prowess of Lucille Clifton. These songs are in conversation with Lucille's poems "birth-day," "homage to my hips," and "what the mirror said."

ACKNOWLEDGMENTS

Thank you to early readers who gave me feedback and talked me through some of my revision woes. Writing a novel takes a village and what a beautiful village I have: Jennifer Baker, Tracey Baptiste, Linda Christensen, Ellen Hagan, Kori Johnson, and Olugbemisola Rhuday-Perkovich.

To my publishing team, especially my editor, Sarah Shumway, and my agent, Rosemary Stimola. And a heart-felt thank-you to Alex Cabal for bringing Nala to life and creating a stunning, fierce cover.